THE WORLD OF
TOLKIEN

MYTHOLOGICAL SOURCES OF *The Lord of the Rings*

THE WORLD OF
TOLKIEN

MYTHOLOGICAL SOURCES OF *The Lord of the Rings*

David Day

CHARTWELL
BOOKS, INC.

The World of Tolkien
by David Day

To Roisin, Aisling and Amy Magill

First published in Great Britain in 2003 by Mitchell Beazley,
an imprint of Octopus Publishing Group Limited

This edition published in 2013 by
CHARTWELL BOOKS, INC.
A division of BOOK SALES, INC.
276 Fifth Avenue Suite 206
New York, New York 10001
USA

ISBN: 978-0-7858-3016-0

Printed and bound in China

Executive Editors: Vivien Antwi and Kate John
Executive Art Editor: Christine Keilty
Project Editor: Naomi Waters
Design: Alexa Brommer
Production: Gary Hayes
Copy Editor: Siobhan O'Connor
Proofreader: Lara Maiklem
Indexer: Catherine Hall

Illustrators: Victor Ambrus (43, 58, 61, 123, 131, 132, 155, 164); Jaroslan Bradac (22, 24, 31, 33, 65, 160); Tim Clarey (1, 29, 54, 109,
112, 115, 116, 119, 156); Alan Curless (42, 91, 114, 134, 172); Gino D'Achille (96, 151, 158, 169, 179); John Davies (108, 157); Sally
Davies (16-17); Les Edwards (139); Michael Foreman (45, 120, 143); David Frankland (32, 88, 163); Neil Gower (27, 64, 83, 84); Melvin
Grant (53, 68, 102, 106, 135, 146, 152); Sam Hadley (9, 39, 59, 76, 80, 95, 124, 137, 166); David Kearney (12, 34, 57, 62, 98, 105, 141,
177); Barbara Lofthouse (2, 49, 50, 101); Pauline Martin (21); Ian Miller (36, 40, 63, 67, 77, 78, 79, 82, 89, 90, 97); Lidia Postma (111);
David Roberts (5, 71, 72, 75, 127, 145).

Extracts are taken from the following works © Tolkien, JRR *The Hobbit* (1937); © Tolkien JRR *The Lord of the Rings* (*The
Fellowship of the Ring* and *The Two Towers* 1954 and *The Return of the King* 1955); © Tolkien JRR *The Silmarillion* (1977);
© "On Fairy Stories" and "Mythopoeia" in Tolkien *JRR Tree and Leaf* (1964); © Tolkien JRR *The Monsters and the Critics and Other Essays*
(1983); © Carpenter, Humphrey and Tolkien, Christopher (eds) *The Letters of JRR Tolkien* (1981); © Carpenter, Humphrey *JRR Tolkien: A
Biography* (1977).

Page 1: Hobbits of the Stoor (left) *and Fallohide* (right) *varieties.*
Page 2: Alqualondë, Elven port of the Undying Lands.
Page 5: The creature Gollum in his underground pool.

CONTENTS

Introduction

As we come up to the 50th anniversary of the publication of *The Lord of the Rings* in 2004, the popularity and enduring appeal of John Ronald Reuel Tolkien continues to grow apace. His trilogy of Middle-earth novels – *The Fellowship of the Ring*, *The Two Towers*, and *The Return of the King* – was recently voted the greatest fictional work of the 20th century, ahead of such luminaries as George Orwell and James Joyce. Peter Jackson's award-winning cinematic adaptations, meanwhile, have broken box-office records around the globe, and brought the world of Middle-earth to life for a whole new generation of fans – and rekindled the magic for older ones.

The World of Tolkien is intended for those fans of the books or the films who want to learn more about the genius behind this awesome creation and the origins of his remarkable ideas. For in his construction of the Middle-earth, Tolkien drew on an enormous range of sources, from the mythological to the historical, the literary to the linguistic, and the personal to geographic. By looking at these, we can both broaden our appreciation of a marvellous author and understand a little more of his intentions.

Tolkien's understanding and appreciation of mythology was second to none, and the more one studies *The Lord of The Rings*, as well as his other works such as *The Hobbit* and *The Silmarillion*, the more this becomes apparent. He draws on *Beowulf* and Anglo-Saxon stories, the language in which he was professor at Oxford. He looks to the Celtic tales, for example, in the history and characters of his Elves. In Norse mythology, the god of Odin acts as a spur for both Sauron the Ring Lord and the wizard Gandalf. Arthurian, Icelandic, and Teutonic tales are touched upon, as are biblical stories and those of ancient Greece and Rome, and likewise Tibetan myths and the legend of Atlantis. The list, as you will discover, is exhaustive.

His historical sources are similarly impressive. In the kingdoms of Arnor and Gondor, for example, Tolkien saw the divided realms of Rome and Byzantium. Like Charlemagne's attempts to reunite these elements in the Carolingian Empire, so it fell to Aragorn to bring together the Dúnedain people. The Elves, like the Hebrews tribes of Moses, are a "chosen people", surviving terrible hardship to reach the "promised land" of the Undying Lands. The mighty war fleets of the Lords of Umbar, not to mention their use of elephants, were comparable to the lords of Carthage.

Tolkien's literary influences, by contrast, had both positive and negative effects. In Melkor, also known as Morgoth the Dark Enemy, Tolkien employed elements of the character of Satan in John Milton's *Paradise Lost*. The *Song of Roland*, that masterpiece of medieval literature, meanwhile, offers inspiration for the last stand of Boromir in his battle with the Orcs on Amon Hen. Tolkien's thoughts on

Shakespeare, on the other hand, were less complimentary. He disliked drama in general, saying that "disbelief had not so much to be suspended as hanged, drawn, and quarterted", and he particularly relished the literary heresy in criticizing the great bard. In his "March of the Ents", which echoes the coming of Great Birnham Wood to Dunsinane in *Macbeth*, and the demise of the Witch-king, which relates to prophesy of Macbeth's own death, Tolkien is rewriting these Shakespearean motifs, as he saw it, for the better.

Language is also a crucial element in the development of Middle-earth. As Tolkien explains in one of his letters, "The invention of language is the foundation … To me a name comes first and the story follows." Tolkien's interest in philology, his work in editing the *Oxford English Dictionary*, his professorships and knowledge of over a dozen languages – all helped to underpin his writing. For example, Tolkien always had a love for the Welsh language, its beauty and its cadence, and it was Welsh that he used as the basis for his Elven languages. Westron, the predominant language of Middle-earth, shares many words with Old English.

Geography also plays it role. Middle-earth, after all, is our Earth, except in an earlier "Myth Time". Tolkien once explained that, in his *Lord of the Rings* trilogy, "the action of the story takes place in the North-West of Middle-earth, equivalent in latitude to the coastline of Europe and the north shore of the Mediterranean". This inevitably draws links with our modern world, as Tolkien goes on to explain: "if Hobbiton and Rivendell are taken (as intended) to be about the latitude of Oxford, then Minas Tirith, 600 miles south, is at about the latitude of Florence".

Finally, the personal also, almost inevitably, plays a role in Tolkien's world. The home of the Hobbits, "The Shire", drew on the rural and pre-industrial English Shires of Tolkien's late Victorian childhood. The village of Hobbiton draws comparisons to the hamlet of Sarehole where Tolkien spent four formative years. He called the hobbit's house "Bag End", which was the name used locally for his Aunt Jane's Worcestershire farm. But it was far more than just his childhood that Tolkien drew on. In the tale of Beren and Lúthien from *The Silmarillion*, for example, he touched on his love for Edith Bratt – a fact reinforced by the engraving of the characters' names on their gravestones.

Whether you are a newcomer to the world of Middle-earth or something of a seasoned fan, this book will, we hope, increase both your enjoyment and appreciation of this great writer. Lavishly illustrated, it is a guide to Tolkien's epic tales and the inspirations that lie behind them. And as impressive and as varied are this vast wealth of sources, it should be noted that in his own creations, Tolkien has risen to become their equal. There is no greater accolade to his genius, perhaps, than the fact that the myths and legends that he created are now so celebrated and widely known.

A World of Language

Tolkien's star

It all began with one star. And from that single light, an entire world was created. In antiquity, it was the "morning star". It was also the "evening star", or the planet we now know as Venus – named after the Roman goddess of love. In 1913, while still a student at Oxford, the young JRR Tolkien discovered that this bright star provoked in him "a curious thrill, as if something stirred in me, half wakened from sleep". What so excited Tolkien was not so much the star itself, but a literary rendering of it in an Old English (Anglo-Saxon) mystical religious poem known as the *Crist of Cynewulf*.

Eala Earendel engla beorohtast – Hail Earendel brightest of angels
Ofer middangeard monnum sended. – Above Middle-earth sent unto men.

As Tolkien was to write later: "There was something very remote and strange and beautiful behind those words, if I could grasp it, far beyond ancient English." From this context, Tolkien deduced that Earendel must refer to the morning star itself, shining as a light of faith above the land of men midway between heaven and hell, otherwise known as "Middle-earth".

Tolkien's excitement was palpable because, in Earendel, "brightest of angels", he believed that he had discovered an original Old English myth. This was the myth behind an obscure fragment of a surviving Icelandic fairy tale: a story about the heroic mariner Orentil, who in Norse mythology was identified with the morning star. Over the next year, Tolkien set himself the task of imaginatively reconstructing what he considered the true myth of Earendel. The end result was Tolkien's composition of a long narrative poem, entitled "The Voyage of Eärendil".

Tolkien's Eärendil – like an ancient Flying Dutchman – is a mariner doomed to wander through an endless maze of shadowy seas and enchanted isles. Transformed into a white seabird Eärendil's beloved Elven princess Elwing brings to him a holy jewel of living light. The hero and his ship are raised to the firmament, where, forever after, Eärendil the Mariner sails the heavens. Upon his brow is the radiant jewel of light that we now see as the morning star.

Tolkien wrote "The Voyage of Eärendil" in the late summer of 1914. Although his poem had its genesis in the lines of another verse, as Humphrey Carpenter describes in his biography of the author, Tolkien had created in Eärendil something uniquely his own – and more besides. As Carpenter puts it, "it was in fact the beginning of Tolkien's own mythology".

Myth and true tradition

Middle-earth and its stories have their roots in Tolkien's love and fascination with language. As he explains in one of his letters, "the invention of language is the foundation... to me a name comes first and the story follows". In the word, to put it another way, was the beginning. As difficult as creating an imaginary world was, constructing a language – complete with its vocabulary, syntax, grammar, and so forth – is an even more arduous task. But throughout his life that is exactly what Tolkien did: from his own pantheon of languages – including Greek, Latin, Lombardic, Gothic, Old Norse, Swedish, Norwegian, Danish, Old English, Middle English, German, and Dutch – Tolkien created over a dozen of his own.

In "The Voyage of Eärendil", later to reappear in various forms in *The Silmarillion* and *The Lord of the Rings*, we have a fantasy inspired by Tolkien's profound understanding of both language and ancient tradition. It was the author's genuine attempt to re-create a story that captured the essential spirit, or "true tradition" of a lost civilization. In order to understand why Tolkien felt so compelled to "reconstruct" an ancient myth, we have to look at the academic discipline that underpinned it: philology.

Philology is the study of the history of languages. Properly known as "comparative philology", it has developed over centuries into a sort of linguistic

Above Tolkien's "reconstruction" of the story of Eärendil the Mariner in the mythology of Middle-earth, is derived from obscure fragments of Icelandic, Anglo-Saxon, and Norse myth.

forensic science, one based on the theories about "laws" which govern all languages. Philologists study phonetic and grammatical patterns in order to create the linguistic equivalent of "genetic fingerprints", allowing languages and people to be traced over the millennia. From just a handful of words from an extinct language, philologists have claimed to discover many previously "lost" civilizations and played a major part in restoring them to their place in the historic record.

Early in his academic life, Tolkien was employed as one of the compilers of the *Oxford English Dictionary* – the largest philological work ever put together. Later, he wrote studies or edited scholarly editions of many of the major Middle and Old English texts. It can safely be said that there were few authors of fiction and poetry in any age who could equal Tolkien's knowledge of the English language. Likewise, there are few who understood so profoundly the deep-rooted meaning and history of words, especially as revealed in the names of people, places, and things.

Tolkien embraced philology with a passion. It provided him with a disciplined means of understanding language structures and gave him profound insights into the evolution of languages and words. It inspired him creatively to investigate languages and words at their most fundamental levels and, most importantly, gave him his theory of "reconstruction". As anthropologists might attempt to reconstruct a lost civilization through fragments of physical evidence, so philologists saw in recovered fragments of languages and literature the possibility of reconstructing the primary myths and, therefore, the cosmos of long-vanished nations.

The "long-vanished nation" that interested Tolkien was the English nation – these were the people of his blood whose ancient myths had been lost. As the English were late in coming to literacy and early in conversion to Christianity, their ancient literature was ignored by the Latin-literate clergy, then ruthlessly suppressed by the Norman French conquerors.

Tolkien believed that "myths are largely made of 'truth', and indeed present aspects of it that can only be received in this mode". He believed it was only through myth that a "glimpse of the underlying reality of truth" of human life could be revealed. He felt that the loss and suppression of their ancient myths and legends meant that the English people had been deprived of their "true tradition". It was these myths, the "primeval jewels of living light" of the English people, that he hoped to recover.

Faith and fairy tales

As a devout Christian whose guardian was a Catholic priest, the challenge of reconstructing these myths created a crisis of conscience for the young Tolkien. After all, the agent responsible for the suppression of his beloved ancestral myths and legends was his equally beloved Church. But Tolkien, as a devout young scholar, hoped that this one bright star was the silver head of the rivet, the rivet that would provide the intellectual justification and moral alibi by which the firmament of pagan mythology might be welded to both the physical universe and the Christian faith. It was within Eärendil's tale that Tolkien believed that he had discovered a means by which his Christian conscience could allow his passion for the pagan mythology to thrive. Like many Christian scholars, Tolkien's alibi was made in the form of finding in ancient mythologies a historic basis for biblical events and ultimately "proof" of the "true myths" of Christianity.

In a series of papers and lectures, *On Fairy Stories*, Tolkien carefully established that he regarded a large body of literature of the human race to be of this ilk: from traditional folk tales to Homer's *Odyssey*, from Spenser's *Faerie Queene* to Milton's *Paradise Lost*. Assuming his professorial role, Tolkien pointed to the essential fairy-story elements. And, although he did not believe that fairy tales and pagan myths were literally true, he did consider them elemental to any sense of national and personal identity, and necessary for the spiritual evolution of the human soul.

The Gospels also contain a fairy story, or a story of a larger kind which embraces the essence of all fairy stories. They relate many peculiarly artistic and moving marvels, mythical in their perfect, self-contained significance. Among them is one of the most complete eucatastrophes (happy endings or joyful consolations). The difference here is that, in the case of the Gospels, the story has entered history and the Primary World. This is the birth of Christ. The Resurrection is the eucatastrophe of the story of the Incarnation. Tolkien sincerely believed that, in the story of Christ, mythology and history met and fused: "Because this story is supreme; and it is true, Art has been verified. God is the Lord, of angels, and of men – and of elves." This was where the importance of ancient myth arose: it was only through the "prefiguration" of miraculous pagan tales that the human imagination could have been prepared to accept the true and historic miracle of Jesus Christ.

In his tale of Eärendil the Mariner, Tolkien believed he had discovered a means of linking his pagan world with a legend already attributed to a Christian saint. From earliest Christian times, the morning star's appearance was linked to John the Baptist, the celebrated "forerunner" of the Messiah. Just as surely as the appearance of this star foretold the coming brilliance of the sun, so the appearance of the spiritual light that was John the Baptist foretold the coming brilliance of the Son of God.

In Tolkien's mind, his mythic world was a "forerunner" to the Christian world wherein the clash of good and evil was the most notable aspect of heroic pagan man. This was the heroic age of his ancestors, and, as with the Christian symbolism that would follow, there is a spiritual light that comes into existence before the coming of the ages of the sun to the mortal world.

Middle-earth revealed

As Tolkien saw it, all that remained of the "true tradition" of the English nation was to be found in the fragments of a few poems and the magnificent *Beowulf*, the only surviving epic of the Anglo-Saxon people. As Old and Middle English were neglected and "contaminated" (as Tolkien saw it) by French and Latin, the "true tradition" had all but vanished. Nothing was left except in the names of places and families, and in the oral traditions of folksong, folklore, and fairy-tales of the English peasantry.

In any Anglo-Saxon text, Tolkien believed, it was through the Old English words that we could understand the difference between our world and the "Middle-earth" of our ancestors. Tolkien suggests that the poet of *Beowulf* saw: "... in his thought the brave men of old walking under the vault of heaven upon the island earth (middangeard) beleaguered by the Shoreless Seas (garsecg) and the out darkness, enduring with stern courage the brief days of life (loene lif), until the hour of fate (metodsceaft), when all things should perish, light and life together (leoht and lif samod)."

This was Tolkien's "glimpse" into the long-vanished world of his ancestors. He wished, however, for more than a glimpse, he wanted the whole of Middle-earth and all its inhabitants. His passion, as he once wrote to a publisher, was for myth, fairy tale, and "above all for heroic legend on the brink of fairy tale and history". Tolkien concluded that the only way he might gain access to such literature would be to create it himself.

Below The only surviving epic of the Anglo-Saxon people, the poem *Beowulf* was a bountiful source for Tolkien's writings. Here, Beowulf enters the waters of Grendel's Mere, infested with sea monsters, on his way to kill Grendel's mother. Similarly, as the members of the Fellowship of the Ring try to enter the Mines of Moria, they are challenged by a many-tentacled, sea-monster who lives in a pool by the Western Gate.

On several occasions Tolkien wrote about his desire to create an entire cosmology based upon his own readings of ancient English history, language, and literature. It was a massive undertaking that he struggled with for his entire life. It was a passion with patriotic intent, for he had often felt sadness at what he considered the literary poverty of the English body of myth and legend when compared with that of other nationalities. He wished to create a body of work that would range from epic poems, to creation myths, fairy tale, and romance which could bear the dedication: "to England; to my country". He wished to create something that seemed born of the soil of England and evoked the air of its rich northern history. He wanted to avoid comparison with the Mediterranean epic tales and cycles and to strike out in a new way more suited to the people and nation that produced one of the most dominant civilizations in the history of the world.

Tolkien's desire to create "a heroic legend on the brink of fairy tale and history" has without doubt been achieved to a degree unmatched by any other author. Tolkien's desire to revive the "true tradition" of his most ancient English ancestors resulted in a heroic romance as brilliant as that "primeval jewel of living light" that shines down from the night sky of Middle-earth. The myths and legends of Middle-earth are arguably now as celebrated and widely known as those of the ancient Greeks, Indians, Chinese, Egyptians, or any other nation of antiquity.

So, from the glimmering light of one star, the ancient lost world of Tolkien's Middle-earth was gradually illuminated and revealed to its creator. As the morning star is the herald of the sun, so beloved by Men; and as the evening star is the herald of the moon, so beloved by Elves, Eärendil is a sign of hope to all on Middle-earth. It was a light that illuminated an ancient world that Tolkien explored for decades and continued to chronicle right down to the last days of his life.

This star was also Venus, the planet of the goddess of love, so it was always a sign of true love. As such it pulls all Tolkien's works of high romance together under one sky. Just as the spark of the star evoked Tolkien's world, so it played its part and glimmered even in the last recorded event in the history of the Elves upon Middle-earth. For these histories conclude with the tale of the last immortal descendant of Eärendil choosing to share the fate of her mortal lover. For her beauty and her doom, she was known to all as Arwen Evenstar, the Evenstar of the Elves of Middle-earth.

Time and Place in Middle-earth

Time in Middle-earth

In his letters of the 1950s, JRR Tolkien wrote several times of the confusion that people felt with regards to the location of Middle-earth. He was frustrated by the fact that people assumed Middle-earth to be on another planet. In fact the name "Middle-earth" was derived from "middle-erd" or "midden-erd", the ancient name for the place where men live, and hence it is part of the real, Primary World.

Where the confusion arises over the place of Middle-earth can be attributed to a misunderstanding over the matter of its location: it is a temporal rather than a spatial issue, a question of not *where* Middle-earth is, but *when*. "The theatre of my tale is this earth," Tolkien explained in one letter, "the one in which we now live, but the historical period is imaginary". That imaginary time is a mythical one just before the first human histories and the rise of any recorded civilization. It begins with the creation of the world known as Arda (Middle-earth and the Undying Lands) within vast spheres of air and light. It is 37,000 years into this history of this particular world before the events described in *The Lord of the Rings* actually begin. After the end of the War of the Ring, it is to be many millennia again before we reach the origins of humankind's ordinary history.

Tolkien himself estimated that our own time starts some 6000 years after the Third Age – in Middle-earth's system, approximately the 20th century of the Fifth or Sixth Age. Working backwards from our own system of time, this would place the War of the Ring at something between 4000 and 5000 BC, and the creation of Arda at 41,000 BC.

This was the real trick of Tolkien's Middle-earth: an imaginary time of the real world's age of myth that had a parallel existence and evolution just before the beginning of the human race's historic time. Tolkien's Middle-earth is meant to be close to what the philosopher Plato saw as the ideal world of archetypes: the world of ideas behind all civilizations and nations of the world. This is a world where all our dreams have their origination.

JRR Tolkien acknowledged that to many men of letters, "fantasy" literature was a highly suspect category – if not totally illegitimate, at least "a childish folly" which a mature reader should avoid. Most of all, they seem to see fantasy or epic romance as a genre which is written and read by those who wish "to escape from the real world". In this respect, Tolkien is not a fantasy writer. Or at least not in the way such categories are usually established. Strictly speaking, he does not make up imaginary worlds or places. Still less does he fit into the category of science fiction, although he does seem to make some major shifts in Einstein's time-space continuum. And, although he quickly dispenses with Darwinian evolution, he seems to be an enthusiastic fan of Lyle's theory of geological evolution. Too enthusiastic, in fact: he puts the theory of continental drift on fast forward – speeding it up by a few hundred million years. The sinking of the island kingdom of Númenor in Tolkien's world causes the flat Mythic World to be transformed into the historic Primary World – our Earth before the beginning of recorded history – and it is this dramatic event that is remembered in the near universal cataclysmic myth of Atlantis. The landmass of Middle-earth then gradually drifts toward the familiar configuration of the continents as we know them today.

So, Middle-earth is not meant to be a "fantasy" at all. Tolkien didn't really read or write "fantasy" fiction to "escape from reality". Quite the opposite, he wrote to learn more about the real world. He studied people and things in life just as he studied words and languages. He would see how they looked and how they sounded. However, to understand words or things deeply, he would insist, one has to see them through time, or better yet, beyond time. One has to look back into their origins and forward towards their final destination. Only then can one understand their essential purpose and spirit.

Tolkien had his own category for what he wrote: mythopoeia. Mythopoeia evoked a sense of wonder in the ordinary, everyday world. Tolkien believed that the Primary World is "made all the more luminous" by the ideal world of myth and fantasy, which reveals the "living light" within each thing. He claimed that it was through fairy tales that he first understood the power of words to evoke the real wonder of basic things: of stones and iron and trees and fire and wine and bread. In writing about the world of myths, Tolkien explained that this realm was not only the dwelling place of dragons and elves, but of ordinary things like grass, the sea, and the sun; and most importantly, it contained us – mortal humans – when we were "enchanted". That is, when we saw beyond the world of simple material being.

Tolkien's point is that we are so often blinded by what becomes commonplace that we lose our sense of what is truly miraculous in life. Through myth and fantasy a sense of wonder rekindles our imagination and sharpens our senses. The archetypal world of myth and fairy tale, Tolkien believed, had not been created to replace reality or escape it. It was a means by which we might truly engage with it. By firing the imagination we may recognize and value what is eternal and true in a fleeting world of appearance. It meant fully engaging with reality: a true and eternal world unconfused by everyday illusions and forms.

By the forging of the magical sword of the dragonslayer, the true wonder of the discovery of cold iron is revealed to us. Through the legend of Shadowfax or

Grani or Pegasus we see true beauty in all horses. In the tales of Trees with Golden Apples of the Sun and Silver Apples of the Moon, the true magical power of all trees, plants, and fruits is discovered.

Tolkien stated that the theatre of the War of the Ring was the north-west of Middle-earth, a region in Myth Time that is analogous to the coastline of Europe and the shores of the Mediterranean. And the Shire of the Hobbits is an analogue for the Shires of the English Midlands on the edge of the Welsh marches. However, as it was a geography in Myth Time, it was shaped by the imagination of a mind something like that of a medieval mapmaker – focused on the familiar lands of the northwest and with a sense of proportion governed by an awareness of the relative importance of one's own homeland.

Place in Middle-earth

In its origins, Tolkien's Middle-earth has much in common with the Midgard of Norse mythology. Here, Midgard, or Middle World, was the central of the three discs or plates set on top of each other. The highest level was Asgard, realm of the

warrior gods, but also Alfheim, the land of the Light Elves. There is similarity here, perhaps, with the Undying Lands. Just as the Undying Lands could only be reached by the magical Elven ships that travelled the Straight Roads, the only way to get to Asgard from Midgard was the flaming rainbow bridge of Bifrost. Midgard itself was home of men, of dwarves, of giants, and of dark elves. It too was surrounded by a vast sea, considered impossible to cross. Beneath Midgard was the third level of Niflheim, the world of the dead – a place not dissimilar to Melkor's Middle-earth during the Ages of Darkness.

In the Change of the World, as Middle-earth changed its shape from flat to globed, Tolkien drew on another myth or, as many have argued, history – that of the ancient kingdom of Atlantis. This is discussed in detail later, in the chapter on the Men of the Second Age, but it is worth mentioning here because of its importance in the structuring of the world of Middle-earth. In the destruction of Númenor, Tolkien sought to re-create the legend of the destruction of Atlantis, thought to be an island about the size of Spain in the Western sea. Númenor, west of Middle-earth is similarly located.

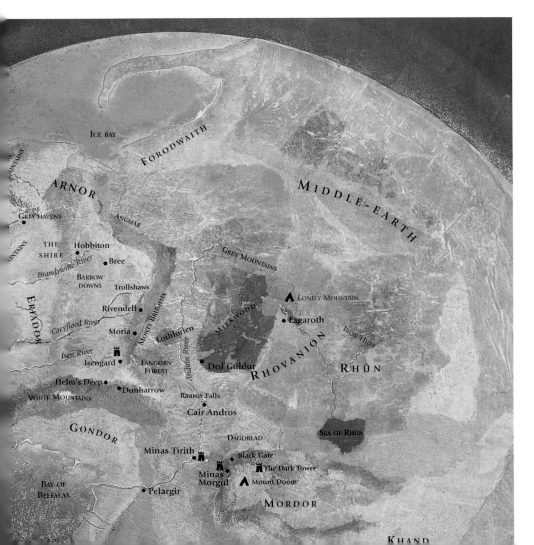

Left Middle-earth is our earth but it exists in an imaginary time. The enchanted Elven ship departs into that timeless dimension of myth to the Undying Lands, and Middle-earth begins to evolve into the globed world just before the "dawn of history".

The fact that Tolkien's Middle-earth predates our own Earth produces a number of exciting and intriguing possibilities as to associations between his world and ours. The knowledge that Tolkien drew on a range of historical as well as mythological sources only serves to increase their resonance. Let us start with "The Shire", which in both essence and latitude can be seen as comparable to England's "green and pleasant land" – a paean to the rural and pre-industrial Shires of Tolkien's childhood. In particular, The Shire is akin to the countryside of the West Midlands, with the village of Hobbiton drawing parallels with the then hamlet of Sarehole (now on the outskirts of Birmingham) where Tolkien spent four formative years of his childhood. As if to enforce the association, Tolkien called the hobbit's house "Bag End", which was the name used locally for his Aunt Jane's Worcestershire farm.

If The Shire is Worcestershire, then the Elven realm of Rivendell can be seen as the equivalent of Oxford. Both are places of scholarly excellence – for the High Elven languages of Quenya and Sindar that are employed in Rivendell, read the ancient Greek and Latin upon which the university of Oxford was founded. They both enjoy a timeless, almost ethereal quality (the "dreaming spires") and are centres of both shelter and counsel. Roughly to the west of Rivendell is the Elven kingdom of Lindon. North and South Lune are bisected by the Gulf of Lune and the Lune River. Here, the comparison is evidently with Wales and Cornwall, which are both west of Oxford, their separation made by the Bristol Channel. Tolkien's association between the Elves and the Welsh, particularly linguistically, was substantial, as we will see later.

Moving slightly further afield, the realms of the Dúnedain draw comparisons with that of the spread of the Roman Empire. Its splitting into the kingdoms of Arnor in the north and Gondor in the south can be seen in essence as the division of the Roman Empire into the West Empire, with Rome as its capital, and the Byzantine East, centred on Constantinople. Indeed, Arnor's division into Arthedain, Rhudaur, and Cardolan mirrors the Roman spheres of Italy, Germany, and France-Spain. As for Gondor, Tolkien suggests a similarity between the overrefined quality of its high culture and the "increasingly sterile" nature of the Byzantine.

In Rhovanion, we can see what the ancient Romans called "Germani": the Great Northern Forest of Europe. In the Horsemen of Rohan, we can draw a link to the supreme horsemen of the Germanic tribes: the Visigoths, Ostrogoths, and Lombards. The Black Land of Mordor, meanwhile, equates with the present-day Black Sea (this fits with the strategic importance of Gondor/Constantinople in controlling the Anduin River/Bosphorus).

This also fits in with the positioning of the ancient port and harbour of Pelargir, at a site equivalent to Troy in modern-day Turkey. In Greek mythology, Troy was founded by the mythic hero Ilus and was most famous for the Trojan War, caused by the abduction by Paris of Helen, who was the wife of the Greek king Menelaus. In Middle-earth, Pelargir acquired an equivalent status as the birthplace of civilization, when Elendil landed his ship here, after the destruction of Númenor.

Further south, we have the wild barbarian lands of Harad, also called the Sunlands, vast and hot with great deserts. The comparison with the heat of Spain and Africa is completed by their inhabitants, the Southrons, whom Aragorn fought just as Charlemagne did the Saracens.

Vast and elaborate as Tolkien's world was, his ambition was not without precedent. In a patriotic attempt to create a Roman rival to the Greek epics, when writing his *Aeneid* Virgil found it necessary to invent almost entirely an ancient mythology around the hero Aeneas, the son of Aphrodite, who survives the fall of Troy and whose descendants founded Rome. After Virgil, this "literary epic" proved to be the most effective means of rewriting history and acquiring famous ancestors. By acquiring Trojan ancestors, the Romans invented a moral alibi for the conquest of Greece and assimilation of the Hellenic Empire. Furthermore, by acquiring Aphrodite as a divine ancestor, Julius Caesar was able to establish his "divine right" to rule as the Emperor of Rome.

The same is true of Geoffrey of Monmouth's *History of the Kings of England* in which Aeneas' great-grandson Brutus appears as Britain's founder and – through his descendent Henry I – the rightful inheritor of the Roman Empire. Similar revisions of history are behind the *Chansons de Gestes*, Spencer's *Faerie Queen*, Malory's *Morte d'Arthur*, and Milton's *Paradise Lost*. In the 19th century, the popular demand for national myths, real or imagined, resulted in a frenzy of "reconstructed" literature: Scott's *Border Ballads*, Grimm's *Fairy Tales*, Tennyson's *Idylls of the King*, Wagner's *Ring of the Nibelung*, and Lonnrot's *Kalevala* in Finland. Tolkien's desire to create "a heroic legend on the brink of fairy tale and history", was achieved. As far as humanly possible, it can be said that the "true tradition" of his ancient English ancestors has been reinvented through the power of Tolkien's imagination, resulting in a body of literature as celebrated as any other nation's mythology.

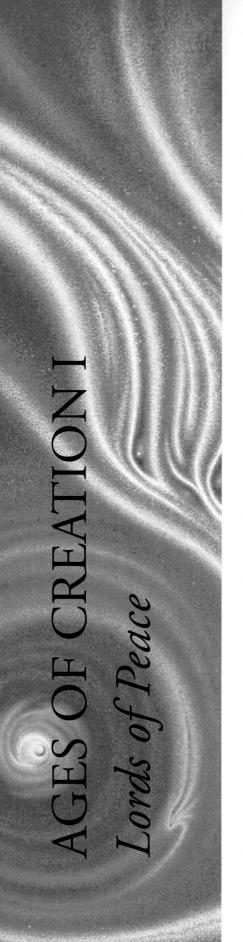

Gods and Deities

The music of Creation

JRR Tolkien once explained how the vast cycle of his tales began with "a cosmological myth: the Music of the Ainur" in which a supreme being and his host of angels sing the world into existence. God in Tolkien's world is known as Eru, The One, or Ilúvatar in the language of Elves. He is an omniscient being living alone in the Void. Those angelic powers, the Ainur, Tolkien explained, should be recognized as: "Beings of the same order of beauty, power, and majesty as the 'gods' of higher mythology."

The sound of the heavenly host leads to the visual entity of the "Spheres of the World". Finally, the sound and the vision are made incarnate by the command and word of Eru: "Eá! the World that Is." (By coincidence, perhaps, Eru has resonance in Greek mythology, as the god of love is Eros and the god of discord is Eris; and Ea in Babylonian mythology is a god of creation.)

Ultimately, in Tolkien's world, music is the organizing principle behind all creation. Tolkien's mystical conception of the World as a manifestation of great musical composition, seems to presuppose a musical cosmos that is an eternally harmonious system created by a Supreme Intelligence. It also presupposes that encoded within the "Great Music" and the "Spheres of the World" is all that was, is, and will be, including the fate of every man and every living thing in creation.

In this, Tolkien is not being so much inventive as entirely consistent with an ancient metaphysical tradition. Tolkien's "Great Music" has its historical precedence in the "Music of the Spheres", the oldest and most sustained theme in European intellectual life. The Music of the Spheres is an all-embracing system of tone and number which gives a logical structure to the universe and has provided the metaphysical structure for most of the world's major religions from Christianity to Islam, from Buddhism to Hinduism.

In most ancient civilizations, the study of music was recognized as the primary means of understanding the universe. Universal among humans is the ability to recognize musically harmonious notes. In the sounding of an octave (two successive "Do's" on a musical scale) there is an abstract, mathematical event that is precisely linked with a physical, sensory perception. Without intellectual training – without interception of thought or image or concept – we immediately recognize the recurrence of the initial tone of the octave. It is the same note, yet different. It is on a different level. Our intuitive, emotional response of sound coincides with an exact intellectual abstract system of measurement.

The key essence of the perception of harmony is that it is the only moment in the created world where the intellectual and the physical world are one. As the Enlightenment rationalist philosopher and mathematician Gottfried Wilhelm von Leibniz (1646–1716) would state two millenia after its discovery, "Music is the hidden arithmetic exercise of a soul unconscious that it is calculating." The codification of the arithmetic basis of music by the brotherhood of the Pythagoreans in ancient Greece was the true beginning of the science. For the first time, man discovered that universal truths could be explained through systematic investigation and the use of logic-based symbols such as those found in mathematics.

So, the inner man and the cosmos could be joined through a universal music. The mind of man could relate to the structure of the universe, and this led Plato to the conception of a "world soul" based on the musico-arithmetic structure of the octave. This philosophically credible conclusion was later transferred to an absolute

Above In the beginning, the great spirits called the Ainur were bidden by Eru, the One, to create a Great Music, out of which came a vision of globed light in the Void.

belief in a musical universe based upon mathematical principles of harmony. And this was the beginning of the quasi-science of astrology.

The stability and existence of the universe were believed to be dependent on harmony: a sympathetic spirit existing between the physical world, the human soul, and the cosmic spirit. Consequently, it was believed that there were three types of music. The first was *musica instrumentalis*: the mathematically precise music of voice and instruments. The second was *musica humana*: the aesthetically true and physiologically simplistic music of the human organism. The third was *musica mundana*: the entirely mystical music of the physical universe. These three types of music, in concert, made up this system of beliefs known as the Music of the Spheres.

In basing his Creation Myth on the "Music of the Ainur", Tolkien was placing his cosmos in a philosophical tradition that was consistent with his faith. The Music of the Spheres not only survived the transition from pagan philosophy to Christian faith, it became one of the most powerful doctrines in the history of the Church.

Ancient pagan gods and the Valar

In Tolkien's adaptation of the Music of the Spheres and especially in his pantheon of his Valarian "Gods", he remains true to this tradition. In the Music of the Spheres there are seven crystal spheres, each governed by the temperament of a particular God, and each related to the other as are the notes in the musical scale. In Tolkien we find there are seven Valar, each of whom controls a major element like air or water or fire, and each has a related temperament which has been predetermined by his part in the Great Music. Working within the created world each must work in concert and in harmony with the others.

In this system, the musical and arithmetic structure of the octave is mirrored in the physical universe: the sun, the moon, and the five visible planets are the seven notes, while the immovable sphere of fixed stars closes the octave. And each has a profound effect on the fate of men and all living creatures. This universe is precisely (and mathematically) tuned like Apollo's seven-stringed lyre, except instead of strings there are crystal spheres – one inside the other. Each sphere hums with a musical tone and each is governed by emotions and powers of the genius of that sphere: Diana the Moon, Apollo the Sun, Mercury, Venus, Mars, Jupiter, Saturn. It is believed that human temperament can be directly affected, and so behaviour becomes Mercurial, Saturnine, Jovial, etc. In some cultures angels or saints govern these spheres, but the principle is the same. Here we have human fate preordained and governed by the stars. The wise man must take care to stay "in tune with the universe". This is the basis of all astrology, ancient and modern.

There are also seven Valier, the female counterparts of the Valar, which doubles the number of musical intervals within the Spheres of the World. This is exactly consistent with the adaptation of fourteen semi-tone system known as the scale of Pythagoras.

In Eru and the Ainur, Tolkien has given us entities comparable to the biblical Jehovah (or Hebraic Yahweh) and his attendant angels. In entering the created Spheres of the World, and becoming the Valar and the Maiar, these entities take on physical forms comparable to the gods and demi-gods of ancient Greek, Germanic, and Norse mythologies. Much was required of these powers when they entered into the Spheres of the World and took on visible forms and domains. In giving individual Vala responsibilities over different realms – the sea, the mountains, and so forth – Tolkien continues this close reference to pantheons of other mythological deities. Like those gods, they were also capable of taking on many different physical forms: god, elf, man, or beast. In earliest ages, the Valar and Maiar are the powers of the earth that shape the World, corresponding to an historic time when forces of nature brought about geological evolution.

Most aspects of Tolkien's history and mythology are temperamentally comparable to the mythology of the northern European Celtic and Germanic races. In his gods, the Valar, however, there are many more parallels with the Greco-Roman pantheon of Olympian gods. Tolkien's High King of the Valar, Manwë, sits upon his throne on the tallest mountain in the world. The eagle is sacred to him and his eyes flash blue with lightening. He is very like the Greek god Zeus – whom the Romans called Jupiter – the king of the gods who ruled from his throne and temple on Olympus, the tallest mountain in his world. The eagle was also sacred to Zeus, the fierce, bearded, blue-eyed god of storms and the thunderbolt.

Manwë's mightiest brothers, Ulmo, the Ocean Lord, and Mandos, the Master of Doom, had direct counterparts in Greco-Roman mythology. Ulmo shares most of his characteristics with Poseidon, the Greek god of the sea – whom the Romans called Neptune. Both were giant, bearded sea lords who drove foam sea chariots pulled by sea horses on the crest of a tidal wave. Mandos shares many characteristics with Hades, the Greek god of the dead – whom the Romans called Pluto. Both were pitiless rulers of the underworld and keepers of the houses of the dead, and both knew the fate of mortals and immortals alike.

Among the goddesses is Yavanna, who is the Queen of the Earth and Giver of Fruits, and her young sister Vána, who is the Queen of Blossoming Flowers. Both the goddesses have direct parallels in the Greco-Roman pantheon. The Greek earth mother and goddess of the harvest is Demeter, whom the Romans called Ceres, while her daughter is the goddess of spring, Persephone, whom the Romans called Proserpine.

Left The Music of the Ainur. The Ainur were individual spirits whose song brought Arda, the Earth, into being at the beginning of time.

In Tolkien's Valarian god Aulë the Smith, we have a counterpart in the Greek god Hephaestus – the Roman god Vulcan. Both were capable of forging untold wonders from the metals and elements of the Earth. Both were supernatural smiths, armourers, and jewellers. Others who are comparable to Greco-Roman gods include Tulkas the Strong, who shares many characteristics with the Greek Heracles (the Roman Hercules), and Oromë the Hunter, who bears a resemblance to the Greek celestial hero, Orion the Hunter.

Trees of silver and gold

So, Tolkien had elaborated his beautiful, musical metaphor of Creation, and his pantheon of Gods. Now he had to establish the manner in which his world would divide day and night. World mythology offered a range of possibilities. The Greek Helios drove a chariot across the sky, drawn by seven cloud-white horses. The Nordic Sunna, in constant flight from Fenris-wolf, symbol of eclipse and darkness, was borne from east to west by three horses. In Egyptian religion, the sun-god Ra was the supreme deity. Surprisingly, perhaps, Tolkien did not incorporate a sun-god into his pantheon. Instead, in a fine conception of his own, his world was initially lit by two mighty lights raised on pillars by the combined power of the Valar. The pillars were placed to the north and south of Middle-earth, and they lasted for five thousand years before crashing to destruction. That was the catastrophe which brought the Earthly Paradise of the Valar to an end: they now withdrew to the non-mortal world beyond the Western Sea.

Here in their new paradisal home, the two pillars were replaced by the Two Trees, sung into being by Yavanna, the earth goddess. One, Telperion, was of silver; the other Laurelin, was of gold. The light they shed corresponded to moon and sun. Again this was a product of Tolkien's own imagination. Trees are well-known in mythology, but not for fulfilling such a function as this. The Nordic legends had Yggdrasil, the "world tree", an ash whose roots and branches bind earth, heaven and hell together. The Celts worshipped various trees, and ascribed special properties to some, especially yew, hazel, and apple. WB Yeats combined the Celtic tradition with the Greek garden of the Hesperides in *The Song of Wandering Aengus*, who sought to:

"…pluck till time and times are done,
The silver apples of the moon,
The golden apples of the sun."

In the Hebraic paradisal garden of Eden there were also two trees, of a fateful nature: the Tree of Life, and the Tree of Knowledge. But Tolkien's light-diffusing trees are unique, serving to remind us that trees play a significant part in our lives. His special feeling for trees will be met again, in discussing the Ents and Huorns.

Later in Middle-earth, as the divine element recedes and the age of Men takes over, we recognize the cosmology we are familiar with today: sun and moon follow their normal courses. One or two stars or planets are mentioned: Borgil, the red planet, Menelvagor the Hunter, presumably Orion. Interestingly, the Moon is masculine, as in German, where it is "der Mond", as it was in Old English.

Although there are many links, both conscious and perhaps unconscious, direct and indirect, between Tolkien's world and the cultures and legends of real past civilizations — and it is a fascinating business to explore them — we should never lose sight of the fact that what really matters is how the author combines them into a single, self-contained system with its own internal coherence and reality. The powerful appeal of the world of *The Silmarillion* and *The Lord of the Rings* is due not to Tolkien's immense knowledge or his command of linguistics, but to his creative genius in constructing a harmonious and believable universe. Much of that is created, and all is shaped, within his own imagination. Without that power of combining, his world would appear an unconvincing assemblage of elements gathered from here and there, and his narrative would lose its grounding in its own reality. As it is, he has succeeded remarkably in creating an original universe and worldscape whose resonances and resemblances to our own and other traditions merely make it even more attractive to the reader.

Left Aulë the Smith, one of the Valar, who were the equivalent of the pantheon of gods of ancient Greece and Rome. Aulë is comparable to the Roman god Vulcan, since his element is the Earth, and he is lord of all craftsmanship with metal and gemstones.

Eagles and Emissaries

Eagle gods and emperors

The Great Eagles of Middle-earth are the emissaries of Manwë, the Lord of the Wind. Looking into Indo-European myths, we find that, where the king of the gods is also the storm god, the eagle is considered the king of birds. Among these nations, the eagle was always one of the heraldic figures representing the king of gods. This also applied to earthly rulers. When Augustus Caesar became emperor of Rome, the imperial eagle was the exclusive property of both Jupiter, the king of gods, and the emperor. The eagle became the standard for the Roman emperor, the Imperial Legions, and the Imperial Government. The imperial eagle was consequently adopted by the Russian czar, the German Kaiser, the Austro-Hungarian emperor, and the self-created French emperor, Napoleon.

Thunderbirds and Valkyries

The Great Eagles of Middle-earth are generally not prominent players in Tolkien's narratives, but their intervention is nearly always crucial, and they are called upon by others at times of desperate need, frequently when in need of rescue from some inaccessible spot. One has a sense that even though they may not be physically present through much of the action, the spirit of these Great Eagles senses all and enables them to turn up just at the critical moment.

Among the North American Indians, the eagle is a powerful heraldic spirit much admired for his swiftness, strength, and courage. As elsewhere, its powers are believed to cause storms and rain clouds. Many Amerindian myths speak of a creature that is part thunder-spirit, part Eagle-spirit. They see at once the spiritual power and physical existence of the bird. This is the thunderbird: its glance is lightning, and its wing stroke is thunder. It flies where it likes and destroys what it wishes.

Among the stories of the Norse and German nations, the role of the eagle is a little more complex, as the king of the gods was Odin, the god of wizards and warriors. His animal companions were the raven and the wolf. Nor was the eagle associated with Thor, the god of thunder. In Norse cosmology, however, the central structure of the universe was Yggdrasil, or the World Tree. On the topmost branch of Yggdrasil is perched an all-seeing eagle, "as the symbol of Odin's sovereignty over the Nine Worlds".

Emissaries of Odin were certainly there, but they were in an unexpected form: the supernatural battle maidens called the Valkyries. Armed with spears of destiny, these beautiful warrior maids in bright armour and gold helms were the

winged angels of fate and luck. As each chosen warrior fell in battle, a shield maiden swept him up and carried him over the Rainbow Bridge. There was also Valhalla, the vast gold-roofed mead hall of Odin, where the heroes are destined to feast and drink until the call to the Last Battle at the End of Time.

Of course, the Great Eagles are just one of several groups of emissaries in Tolkien's world. Some of the other Valar had their own affiliated creatures, and many other emmissaries dwelt in forest and under hill, near rivers, and on mountain ranges. In *The Lord of the Rings*, we find the most the most important emissaries were the Istari, the Wizards. Their purpose was to inspire spirits in the fulfilment of their destinies. Like the Valkyries, the Great Eagles are sometimes the divinely chosen vehicles of destiny, an interloping *deus ex machina*.

Above Having completed their task and destroyed the One Ring, the Hobbits, Sam Gamgee and Frodo Baggins lay exhausted at the foot of Mount Doom as fire and devastation raged all around them. Just in time, Gwaihir, Windlord of the Eagles of Middle-earth, and Meneldor the Swift swoop down and carry the Hobbits to safety.

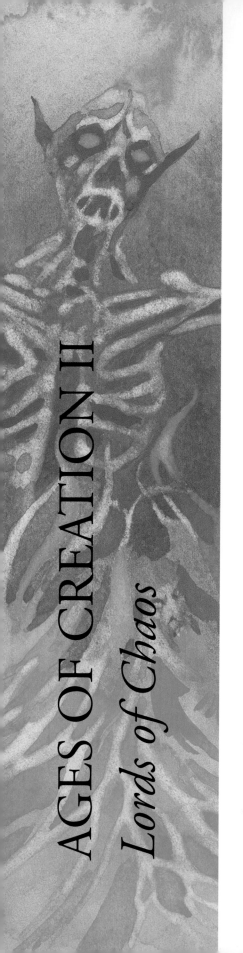

Morgoth – the Dark Lord

In the histories of Middle-earth, there were only two iron-willed tyrants who assumed the title of "Lord of Darkness" and brought all forces of evil into a single alliance. In *The Lord of the Rings* this tyrant was manifest in the fiery Evil Eye of Sauron the Necromancer. By his mastery of the dark fire, Sauron became the Lord of the Rings, and the Dark Lord of Middle-earth. However, the eldest and greatest Lord of Darkness was of the highest rank of angelic powers, whose music shaped the World. This was Melkor or "He Who Arises In Might", the Rebel Vala and First Dark Lord.

In Tolkien's not-yet Christian world, Melkor in one sense parallels Lucifer, the fallen archangel, who personifies the principle of evil. But again Tolkien's imaginative course diverges on its own line. There are no humans yet for Melkor to seduce and corrupt. The theological subtleties and difficulties of Original Sin are wisely avoided. Instead he exists as a negative force, seeking to undo whatever good is done. His "creations" are warped things, not true beings, but hideous parodies of elves, dwarves and others.

Evil in the world of Tolkien is a personal quality – within the freedom provided to beings of godlike intelligence and power, Melkor chose to rebel and to oppose. Once that choice was made, other things followed. To retreat from evil is difficult if not impossible: none of Tolkien's major wicked characters shows any sign of regret or repentance. Rather, it is always easy for a good person to slip – Boromir of Gondor, who tries to take the Ring from Frodo, for good motives, is a prime example. His weakness is the same as Melkor's, pride that prevents him from seeing things, and himself, in their right perspective.

As a fallen angelic power who provokes a war between "heaven and hell", Melkor-Morgoth most resembles Lucifer-Satan, the Fallen Angel of the Judeo-Christian tradition. In his use of biblical language and description of battles between the forces of "heaven and hell", John Milton's magnificently rebellious Satan in *Paradise Lost* has much in common with Morgoth and his many wars with the Valar, the Angelic Powers of Arda. In the cosmology of the ancient Greeks, there were the Wars of the Gods and the Titans, where the giant Titans of the earth arose to fight the gods; and in this conflict, mountain ranges rose and seas fell. Ultimately, the titanic forces of the earth were conquered and forced back underground, just as they were during the wars of the Valar.

Why could the Ainur not be allowed to compose their own music and bring forth life and worlds of their own? This was Melkor's complaint, that he would have freedom from tyranny over his spirit and his creations, just as Lucifer proclaimed in defiance of Jehovah in *Paradise Lost*.

It was Lucifer, the "Bringer of Light", who was cast down from his place in heaven to his pit to become the hell-bound Satan the "Prince of the World". Similarly Melkor's downfall resulted in his creation of his own kingdom in the fiery pits and caverns of Angband ("hell of iron") and his assumption of the Satanic shape of Morgoth the Enemy. Both are loud in their defiance, claiming they would "rather rule in hell than serve in heaven". One might have admired these rebel angels if one believed their defiance was in the name of liberty – however, both lied. Their rebellions were only provoked by envy and the usurpers' wishes to take the perceived tyrants' place. Never were there two more natural tyrants than Morgoth and Satan.

Morgoth can also be found in the tales of the ancient Goths, Germans, Anglo-Saxons, or Norsemen, where similar sorts of Giants, ultimately overthrow the gods and bring the world to a cataclysmic end known as Ragnarok or Gotterdammerung. Melkor-Morgoth can be seen in the darkest aspects of both the king of the gods, Odin, and the king of the giants, Loki. Loki the Trickster, was the embodiment of Discord and Chaos. Odin was king of the gods, and in some ways is

Below In Milton's *Paradise Lost*, Satan emerges from a lake of fire. He is a ruthless, magnificent anti-hero, much like Melkor, the "fallen" Vala of Tolkien's world of Arda.

Right Once Melkor assumed his evil form permanently he became known as Morgoth, the "Dark Enemy of the World". His face was scarred and twisted with rage, and he wore heavy black armour.

comparable to the two Olympian gods Zeus and Hermes. However, Odin had his terrifying aspect, linking him with the Elvish name "Mor-goth", meaning "Dark-Enemy", but suggestive of the "Black-Goth" God, whom Tolkien called "Odin the Goth, the Necromancer, Glutter of Crows, God of the Hanged."

Events after the downfall of Melkor also bear resemblance to early creation stories of ancient Greek mythology. Here, Chaos became two things divided: Uranus the Sky and Gaea the Earth. Gaea gave birth to the Seven Titans and their spouses, but Uranus cast them down into Tartarus. Yet a Seventh Titan, known as Cronos or Time, rebelled and ended Uranus's tyranny over the Earth by castrating the deity with a Sickle. And so, in one swift stroke Time began upon the Earth. For mortals and immortals alike, within the Spheres of the World, there is the terror of the swinging Sickle of Time. For, whether it comes too soon or too late, there is no escape. For the doom of all is contained within its rhythm and even Cronos was in time overthrown.

Similarly, after Melkor was overthrown the march of Time began that would thereafter run upon the world and the sickle motif is repeated. And "High in the north as a challenge to Melkor, Varda the Queen of the Stars set the crown of seven mighty stars to swing, Valacirca, the 'Sickle of the Valar' and a sign of Doom." Discord would no longer be tolerated; the Great Music was the order of the universe. To be out of tune with the Music was to be out of tune with Nature. Everyone had his allotted place in this system. In historic time this structure and philosophy was called the Music of the Spheres and codified in the "Great Chain of Being". But some, such as Milton's Satan and Tolkien's Melkor, saw this Great Chain of Being as the chain of slavery.

Sauron – the Ring Lord

In *Morgoth's Ring* JRR Tolkien and his editor Christopher Tolkien attempt to differentiate between the two Dark Lords; thus defining two categories of evil: Domination and Destruction. The evil of Sauron as the Lord of the Rings was far weaker in its overall power, but far more focused and efficient. This evil of the Necromancer crushes the will and overwhelms the mind of an enemy. Its purpose was Domination. Conquest meant enslavement of the mind, and submission of the spirit of all to the tyranny of the Dark Lord of Mordor. The Master of the One Ring wished to become Eru the One upon Middle-earth. However, Sauron lacked the power to grant his creatures independence of will. Sauron's creatures, like the Ringwraiths, had immense powers of control over the minds and wills of their foes, but they themselves were Sauron's slaves in their every action, and they barely existed except as terrifying phantoms; lethal extensions of the Ring Lord's immortal desire to enslave all life.

There is a hint of Mary Shelley's Baron von Frankenstein about Tolkien's evil sorcerors such as Morgoth, Sauron, and Saruman. This similarity is because of their

Right The god Odin from Norse mythology is a likely source of inspiration for Tolkien's Ring Lord Sauron. Odin too wielded a ring of power, named Draupnir, which held sway over the bearers of lesser rings of power.

failed attempts to usurp the life-creating authority and power of God-Eru. This usurption of power can only produce monsters that are a mere imitation of life. These are creatures that are by their very nature without a moral conscience and without free will. In the end, they can only serve an evil master – though even evil intent can sometimes turn to good purpose.

The Ring Lord and mythology

Throughout his fictional writing, Tolkien employs the literary device of inventing a "prototype story", an earlier "true event" that helps to explain later well-known tales and legends of nations. In *The Lord of the Rings*, he is attempting to create the archetypal ring-quest cycle on which all others are based. The truth, of course, is that, in the character of Sauron the Ring Lord and his quest for the One Ring, Tolkien drew on a wealth stories – Celtic, Greek, German, and Tibetan among them. The sagas with the strongest association, however, and perhaps the closest to the story of Sauron, are the Viking myths and legends, and in particular those involving the Vikings' supreme god, Odin.

God, sorcerer, warrior, trickster, transformer, necromancer, mystic, shaman, king – no figure in mythology is closer to Sauron than that of Odin. Both acquired mastery over wolves and birds – ravens in Odin's case, crows in Sauron's. Odin's desire for dominion over the Nine Worlds matches Sauron's thirst for control of Middle-earth. Their intentions were identical: to gain control of a magical, all-powerful ring: the One Ring in the case of Sauron, Draupnir for Odin. Just as the One Ring combined the talents of Sauron and the Elf Celebrimbor, so the Nordic ring was a combination of the skill of the elfs Sindri and Brok, and all the wisdom of Odin. Just as the One Ring controlled all the other Rings of Power, so Draupnir dripped eight other rings on every ninth day, which Odin gave out to others to govern for him.

As well as the similarities to be found in the characteristics and sources of power of Odin and Sauron, both Odin and Sauron's stories are dominated by their quest for their One Ring. Just as Sauron lost his ring in the war with the Last Alliance of Elves and Men, so Odin lost his at the funeral of his favourite son, Balder. As his son's funeral ship was set alight and consumed in flames, Odin placed Draupnir on Balder's breast. Like Sauron, Odin's power was diminished without the ring. Like the One Ring, however, Draupnir was not destroyed, but went with Balder into the dark realm of Hel, the prison of the dead. And like Sauron sending out his Black Riders to recover the ring, so Odin mounted his eight-legged steed Sleipnir, in order to reclaim Draupnir.

There is a third striking comparison between Odin and Sauron, and that is the motif of the single, solitary eye. We have seen already how in the Third Age

Sauron takes the form of a fiery, evil eye. In the Norse canon, we have Yggdrasil, the great ash tree also known as the World Tree, whose mighty limbs support the Nine Worlds. At Yggdrasil's foot is the Fountain of Wisdom, and it was there, thirsty for knowledge, that Odin went to drink. For one deep draught from the Fountain, Odin had to sacrifice an eye, which he did without hesitation. From that time on, he was always the One-Eyed God.

Although the most obvious, Odin is not the only mythological figure with relevance to Sauron. In Celtic myth, there is the character of Balor the Evil Eye, the king of a monstrous race of deformed giants called the Formors. Balor had two eyes, but only one was normal. The other was huge, swollen, and kept shut because it had been filled with such horrific, sorcerous powers that it virtually incinerated whomever and whatever it looked upon.

In the Tibetan epic of Gesar the Ling roams Kurkar, evil sorcerer and King of Hor. Kurkar has a huge iron mandala ring, or talisman, from which he derives his power, and like the One Ring, it is deemed almost indestructible. As the volcanic power of Mount Doom is required to destroy the One Ring, so Gesar the Ling summons his supernatural brothers and a multitude of spirits to build a great furnace, with "coal piled high as mountains".

Below As the fabled ring of the Tibetan sorcerer, Kurkar, could only be destroyed by a great furnace so too could the Ring of Power only be destroyed in the fires of the Crack of Doom.

Two further myths should also be mentioned. In Sauron's appearance as Annatar, there is something of the Titan Prometheus from ancient Greece. Prometheus, too, had the skills of a master smith, and, just as Annatar offered to share his skills with the Elves of Eregion, so the deity Prometheus shared his with humankind. It was a decision that infuriated the other gods, who bound and enslaved Prometheus as a result, until Zeus decided to break his chains, filling one of the broken links with a fragment of rock, to create the first ring.

Furthermore, in the end of Sauron, there are similarities with the German legend of Dietrich von Berne and the Ice Queen. In his battle with Janibas the Necromancer, Dietrich sees that Janibas's power derives from an iron tablet. When Dietrich lifts his sword and smashes the iron tablet, the glaciers of the mountains split and shatter, thundering down in massive avalanches that bury the entire evil host forever. The result of the destruction of the iron tablet on Janibas's evil legions is identical to that visited on those of Sauron following destruction of the One Ring.

Balrogs – Regions of Flame

Balrogs and the fire giants of Muspellsheim

The most terrible of the corrupted spirits who became the servants of Melkor were the Maiar fire demons, or "Balrogs". Of all Melkor's creatures, only the Fire-breathing Dragons of the Ages of the Sun were considered greater in power. Although Balrogs were known to carry the mace, axe, or flaming sword, their chief and most feared weapon was the many-thonged whip of fire. Tolkien's Balrogs were wild and destructive fire demons, not unlike the Furies, the enraged spirits of vengeance who had snakes for hair and carried flaming torches and used whips to beat their victims.

In many mythologies, there are evil volcanic spirits who live like the Balrogs deep in the roots of mountains. Medieval Christians often saw volcanoes as the vents of the fires of Hell. For the ancient Greeks and Romans, volcanoes were perceived as fires of the smith god Haephaestos (or Vulcan), where the wild spirits of earth and fire were tamed or enslaved by the Olympian gods and turned to more useful purposes at the forge.

Tolkien appears to have been greatly impressed by the fire spirits found in Norse and Anglo-Saxon mythology. Their Midgard was a "Land of Men" which was similar to Tolkien's Middle-earth. Northern Midgard was closed in by a land of frost Giants, while the south was a land of fire giants. This demonic land of fire was called

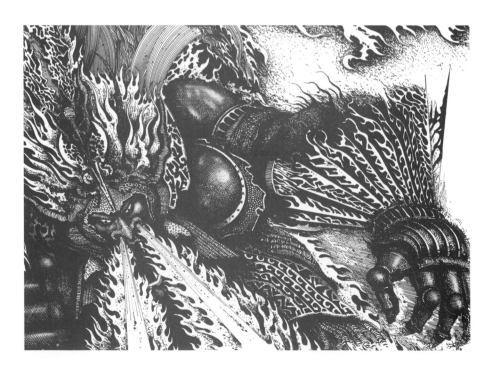

Right Balrogs were evil monsters in the service of Melkor. Dwelling deep inside fiery mountains, they are akin to the fire spirits found in Anglo-Saxon and Norse mythology.

"Muspellsheim". It was Muspellsheim that most provoked Tolkien's imagination in his creation of his extraordinary demons of fire, the Balrogs.

In Norse mythology, we find that, on the border of Muspellsheim, there crouched a giant guardian who was armed with a great sword of flame. Perhaps a coincidental hellish antithesis to the Bible's archangel Michael, with his righteous sword of flame, this guardian of the fiery gates of Muspellsheim was known as Surt, the lord of fire. Ever watchful, Surt awaited the sound of Heimdall, the god of light, blowing Gjall, the horn of the gods, to call forth Odin and the other gods to Ragnarok, or Gotterdammerung. This was the apocalypse, the ultimate battle at the end of the world, and Heimdall was the giant guardian of the Rainbow Bridge that crossed the heavens in the land of the gods.

At the sound of the great horn's blast, Surt, with his sword of flame, leads the sons of Muspell, who "will form a host in themselves and that a very bright one", into battle, wherein Surt, the lord of fire, will duel with Freyr, the god of sun and rain, and patron of bounty and peace. The Rainbow Bridge is destroyed as Surt's flames rain down from the heavens. In the conflagration, the gods, the giants, and the world will be totally consumed in flames.

In *The Silmarillion*, at the end of the War of the Great Jewels when the host of Valinor came to make war on Morgoth in Beleriand, we find a close parallel of narrative detail to this Norse battle of Ragnarok. Tolkien's battle also begins with the blast of a horn, the Horn of Eönwë, the Herald of the Valar. At its sounding a fiery demon, the Balrog, Gothmog, also joins battle, just like Surt at Ragnarok. And finally, as a result of this battle, Morgoth and all his servants, including most of the race of Balrogs, are destroyed, just as the Norse battle results in the final destruction of the world.

Battle on the Rainbow Bridge

The shamanic cultures of all northern European and Asian cultures who use iron and steel weapons claim "the sorcerer and the smith come from the same nest". Both are acknowledged as alchemists and named "masters of fire". However, it is the source of that fire that determines their nature and purpose. Sauron's One Ring was forged in the "dark fire" of Morgoth the Enemy. This gave the Ring Lord command over all the satanic fires beneath the Earth.

But Gandalf also wields the power of fire, the celestial fire of Eru. In the duel of Gandalf with the Balrog, we see a battle between the two kinds of alchemical fire, the white and the dark, vividly illustrated. The Wizard's battle with the Balrog of Moria once again mirrors the Norse myth of the Ragnarok. In *The Lord of the Rings*, the Balrog of Moria with his sword of red hot fire duels with Gandalf the Wizard

Right The wizard Gandalf turns to face his mighty enemy, the Balrog of Moria, on the Bridge of Khazad-dûm in a contest that bears close resemblance to the struggle between Surt and Freyr on the Rainbow Bridge in the climactic battle at the end of time in Norse mythology.

with his sword of cold white flame on the narrow stone bridge over the chasm of Moria. This is a diminished form of the titanic struggle between Surt and Freyr on the Rainbow Bridge. Both battles begin with the blast of a Great Horn: the Norse Horn of the Aesir, blown by Heimdall; and the Horn of Gondor, blown by Boromir. Also, both battles seem to end in disaster –both bridges collapse, and both sets of combatants hurtle down into a rage of flame to their doom.

The encounter between Gandalf and the Balrog is a breaking-point in more than one way. Literally, of course, the stone bridge collapses as the wizard is dragged down into the abyss. The Fellowship of the Ring is broken by the loss of its guide and mentor. The wizard's life is assumed by his friends to be ended. And the quest itself is taken beyond a point from which there can be no return. They can only go onwards now. It is a bravura example of Tolkien's art as a story-teller: to do away (apparently) with a key character in the middle of the action is a bold stroke. It also illuminates the modern, moral dimension of Tolkien's world, which separates it from the great epic narratives of earlier times. In *The Iliad*, when Hector is slain by Achilles, it is a forewarning of the doom of Troy. Siegfried's murder in the *Nibelungenlied* presages the calamity that will befall all the Nibelungs. But the removal of the supernatural Gandalf is an opportunity for the merely human, Elvish, Dwarvish, and Hobbitish characters of *The Lord of the Rings* to display their resilience and courage and rescue themselves from an apparently hopeless situation.

Great Spiders – Regions of Dark

The unlight of Ungoliant

It is difficult to create something as deeply unpleasant as JRR Tolkien's Ungoliant, the Great Spider. She represents more than the simple physical horror of gigantic, unnatural arachnids bent on something worse than murder. What she does represent might best be described as crawling, animated, moral black holes in space. Ungoliant was all the deadly sins incarnate at once, with one evil thing (and one leg) to spare. In this creature, Tolkien discovers a dark horror and substance that he names "Unlight". This is an accurate description, and something that makes her many times more fearful and shocking because she is female. It is hard to imagine the reproduction of this creature, as it involves the production of more "Unlight", of these sucking black holes, so in fact it must be seen as some kind of "Unbirth". If Ungoliant had any sort of birth at all, it seems likely that she was originally a corrupted Maia spirit, a manifestation of Morgoth's evil spirit growing apart from him in darkness and cold. Whatever she was, she was a prophecy of his destiny. In Ungoliant, Morgoth unleashed something beyond evil and beyond darkness.

Kali – destroyer of the world

Perhaps only on the Indian subcontinent is there a mythological creation that comes close to Ungoliant. She is an eight-limbed being known as Kali the Black One. Kali, the Hindu goddess of destruction, also took other names and other forms, but in her eight-limbed form known as the Black One she was seen to dance on the slaughtered body of her lover. Kali the Black One's most notorious cult was that of the Thugees, or "Stranglers", who, using a cord or wire loop to garotte or choke their victims, sanctified the acts of murder and robbery. The murdered bodies of some victims were given up to Kali's priesthood, while others were kept captive alive so that they might later have their hearts ritually cut out. By the early 19th century, the British Army is believed to have eliminated the cult of the Black One and the Thugees – from which the English word "thug" was derived.

Above all, Kali was the "Destroyer of the World". Nothing gave her joy except destruction. As Kali the Black One, she ate only raw meat. She demanded blood sacrifices, intoxicating drink, and ritual suicides. In her dances of death, Kali brandished weapons with each of her eight hands. Into her court came evil men, murderers, all wicked spirits, vampires, wizards, and zombies. To her court also came the "bhuta", the spirits of all who died a violent death. For them, and others, Kali the Black One would perform her dances of death. Sometimes she would dance over the bodies of her slaughtered consorts. At other times she would dance to demonstrate "the power of death at the end of the world" which, ultimately, cannot help but be a dance of self-annihilation.

Few cultures have really grasped the concept of nonexistence as have Indian and Tibetan cultures. And even among many there, it is denied as a logical absurdity. If one looks to the Upanishads: "How could Being be born from Non-Being? Oh, my beloved, Being alone existed in the beginning, Being unique, second to none." In the Tibetan Painted Scrolls, however, we find a "Master of Non-Being" of similar temperament to Kali the Black One (and also to Ungoliant) and in a curiously familiar form.

The Master of Non-Being in the Tibetan Painted Scrolls strongly resembles Melkor the Dark Lord. Furthermore, in his deeds, the Master of Non-Being achieved almost identical acts of destruction. Known only as "Black Hell", this creature was a living form of darkness. A huge entity, his scorched black form was the traditional colour of demonic sorcery. The Master was a "Black Man, as tall as a spear… This man was the Master of Non-Existence, of instability, of murder and of destruction." Demons swarmed about him, and all others fled. "He made the sun and the moon die and assigned demons to the planets and harmed the stars."

Arachnids through history

One wonders if Professor Tolkien shared the common human aversion to spiders. Certainly arachnids play a prominent and unfriendly part both in *The Hobbit* and *The Lord of the Rings*, as well as in earlier Middle-earth history. Clearly Tolkien knew enough of the natural history of the spider to be aware that the female is the active and usually dominant gender. Some commentators have even gone so far as to interpret Tolkien's portrayal of the Shelob episode in particular as evidence of a latent mysogyny.

Spiders have not always had a bad press. Robert Bruce, king of Scotland, was famously inspired by one at a low point in his fortunes. Another spider spun its web across the mouth of a cave where the Prophet Mahomet was hiding; and his pursuers passed it by. Their industry has often been praised. They have even been supposed to have medicinal qualities: in England, jaundice sufferers were once made to eat a large spider trapped in butter. And yet, many find something chilling in the posture, form and movement of the spider. Whether or not he was tapping into a private phobia of his own, Tolkien's depiction of the vast spider lurking in her claustrophobic tunnels is for many readers perhaps the most spine-chilling episode in the Ring trilogy.

Above It is not just in the number of her limbs that Kali bears resemblance to the Great Spiders of Middle-earth. In her black incarnation, Kali is a bloodthirsty killer, just like Ungoliant, the first of the Great Spiders.

Left Ungoliant, in allegiance with Melkor, destroys the Trees of the Valar in the Undying Lands, and consumes their light.

Wolves and Vampires

Slayers who hunt in the night

The Dark Lord had many loyal servants who, like the Valar, could take on any form they wished; most of them assumed the forms of the great wolves who hunted at night. There were also those who chose the form of the giant vampire bats. These creatures were also skin changers who attacked their enemies in the dark and sucked the blood of their victims.

Belief in lycanthropy and vampirism is as ancient as the human race: there are records of these practices as far back as ancient Egypt. The transformation of humans to animals and animals to humans has been a part of every shamanic culture. There was a cult dedicated to Zeus the Werewolf operating in Arcadia in Socrates' time. Throughout the Middle Ages, the belief in vampires in the form of bats sucking the blood from human victims was particularly common.

It was not until the twentieth century that European zoologists actually caught up with the human imagination by discovering one bat species in South America that did, indeed, drink blood. "Lycanthropy" and "vampirism" became terms used in psychiatry as well as folklore, usually as a metaphor for a psychological state. Still, among human cultures, there are traditions where both drinking blood and cannibalism were practised as a means of terrifying enemies and terrorising subjects into submission.

Elements of these traditions can be found in Tolkien's work, from the smallest to the largest. The Flies of Mordor – grey, brown, and black creatures marked with a red eye shape on their backs – traverse the kingdom in bloodsucking swarms. In the "Quest of the Silmaril", Thuringwethil, the "woman of secret shadow", was a giant vampire with massive wings and iron-clawed talons with which she could rip her prey. In another incident, Sauron changed from werewolf to that of a vampire bat, so that he might take flight and find refuge in the deep pits of Angband.

Guardians of hell

In Norse mythology, the heraldic beast of Odin, the one-eyed Necromancer and father of the gods, was the wolf. As Odin was the god of battles, Odin's beasts were creatures who always profited from war. When Odin presided in the Hall of the Slain, at his feet lay his bodyguards: two great wolves, one whose name was "Fear", the other whose name was "Pain". But by far the most terrifying wolf in Scandinavian legend was Fenris, brother of Hel, god of the underworld. His opened jaws touched heaven and earth. Kept in fetters, when Ragnarok, the destruction of

Right Sauron wielded power over an evil race of Werewolves, just as the Wolf was one of the servant-creatures of his counterpart, Odin, in Norse mythology.

Below Large or small, all bloodthirsty creatures were in the thrall of the evil lord Sauron. The flies of Sauron even bore the symbol of his eye upon their backs.

the gods, came at last, he would break out of them and devour Odin himself; while the earth would be overwhelmed by the sea, and all living things would perish

In *The Silmarillion*, the greatest wolf legend is about Carcharoth, the unsleeping guardian of the Gates of Angband; none could pass him by strength of body alone. In this wolf guardian of the Gates of Angband, we can see parallels with other guardians at the gates of the dead in other mythologies, such as the Norse Garm, the hound guardian of Helheim, and the Greek three-headed Cerberus, the monstrous watchdog of Hades.

Carcharoth eventually meets the one who was doomed to slay him: Huan, the Wolfhound of the Valar. And, though he bit Huan with venomous teeth by which the hound would also perish, Carcharoth was at last slain by that Hound of Heaven. And so was told the tale of the "Hunting of the Wolf", which took on an epic scale and found its counterpart in that famous Greek legend of the Calydonian boar hunt. In the Greek story, Oeneus, the king of Calydon, failed to pay homage to Artemis, goddess of the wild, in the annual sacrifice to the gods, and Artemis responded by unleashing on his kingdom the largest, most savage boar anyone had seen. The boar killed men and livestock, and destroyed crops, until Oeneus called for the bravest to come to kill the boar, with the creature's skin the prize. Many came and were killed by the boar, but finally the huntress Atalanta drew blood, and the King's son Meleager finished the battle with his hunting spear.

In contrast to the wolf-monster, there is the tamed dog, friend to man and fellow-hunter. The tale of the hound faithful unto death is a favourite one in ancient literature, and goes back to Sanskrit texts. The wolf Carcharoth met its end when it was killed by Huan, the great wolf-hound of the Valar. Yet in slaying the wolf, Huan himself was doomed to die, poisoned by the beast's venomous teeth. Again Tolkien gives an original twist to a familiar theme. He would certainly have been well acquainted with the story of Gelert, favourite hound of the Welsh prince Llywelyn. Gelert had saved Llywelyn's baby from a savage wolf, but the prince entering and seeing nothing but an overturned and blood-spattered cradle, killed the dog before finding the baby alive and the wolf dead. The hound and the giant wolf are very much part of Tolkien's epic machinery, elements introduced in his tale to confirm its lineage – even, one might almost say, its precedence – in a long Indo-European narrative tradition. But otherwise, dogs, and cats for that matter, do not figure in the tales. In fact, apart from wolves, bears and horses, Tolkien's Middle-earth is somewhat lacking in animal life.

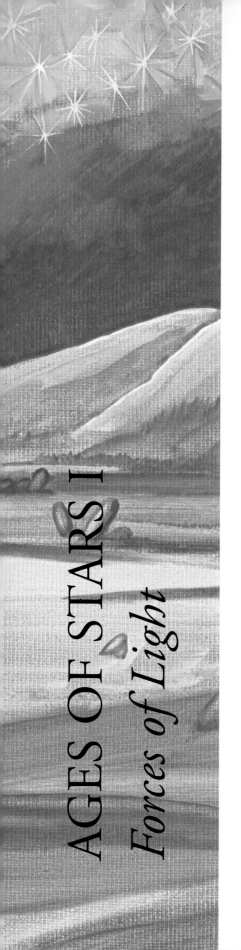

Lands of the Elves

The awakening of the Elves

Eru Iluvatar sent the Valar into the World to prepare for the coming of his Children: Elves and Men. Conceived in the Music of Ainur, the place and time of the awakening of the Children of Iluvatar were hidden. This history of the world of the Elves is akin to the idea of the ancient philosophers of Greece who believed that all things were conceived as thoughts first perceived as music. Tolkien presents Eru the One (with his angelic choir) as the creator-composer-conductor of his own variation of the Music of the Spheres. The Music of the Spheres was an aesthetic science and philosophy that was taught in Europe for over 3000 years – right up until Tolkien's youth at the beginning of the twentieth century. Music was central to any serious education; particularly in its theoretical form. It was in such a musical universe that the First Children were created. These were the Elves. They were created in the mind of the One, then shaped in the pure undulations of the Music of the Ainur. However, they slept until they were awakened by a pure light of "living silver" when Varda, the Lady of the Heavens, gathered the 'living silver' dew of the Trees of the Light, and with that blessed light set the stars ablaze above the world.

Tolkien's Elves are immortal, with far greater skills, intelligence, strength, and endurance than humans. Indeed, Tolkien knew that belief in Elves was widespread among the ancient Anglo-Saxons and early Germans as far back as any records survive. The Anglo-Saxons called them "Aelf" or "Ylfe", and the Norsemen knew them as the "Alfar" or "Alfr", while in Old High German they were "Alp" and in Gothic "Albs"; the only difficulty is that there is little in the way of consistency in their definition. Curiously, the first Irish name recorded by the Romans for Celtic Britain was Albion – meaning either: "elfland" or "whiteland". As Tolkien was also well aware, Albion was the name for ancient Britain used by poets and mystics such as William Blake. In early drafts of *The Silmarillion*, it was the ideal of Albion that motivated Tolkien (unsuccessfully) to attempt to merge the Isle of the Elves and its port of Avallónë with the mythology and history of the British Isles.

The Icelanders and Old Norse texts refer to the "light elves" and the "dark elves", but also name a race of "black elves" (or "swart elves") who live in a subterranean "Svartalfheim" and who seem virtually interchangeable with the Norse references to dwarfs, gnomes, demons, and giants. Tolkien insisted on clarifying definitions and forms of language, by making "Elfs" become "Elves" and "Elfin" become "Elven". Tolkien wished to define the "Elf" as a distinct and singularly important species. In many languages Elf means "white" (the Latin "alba" and Greek "alphos" both mean

"white"), and the word also retains an association with "swan". It is through tracing back to the roots of language that Tolkien's Elves emerged from their ancient past. *The Silmarillion* is a record of over 30,000 mortal years in the evolution of a small part of Elvish history. Tolkien's great migration of the Elves is in large part a means of giving definition to the Elves from a multitude of lost traditions and mythologies that had been reduced by the passage of history to descriptions of a single word: light, dark, green, gray, sea, sylvan, river or wood. Tolkien came to the rescue of these long-lost nations and brought them to life again in the pages of literature. In the writing of *The Lord of the Rings* and *The Silmarillion*, Tolkien gave life and context to the long histories of over forty races, nations, tribes and city-states of Elves.

In *The Silmarillion*, Tolkien gives an account of their creation and awakening in the east of the mortal lands of Middle-earth. For a long time, the Elves dwelt in the east beneath the stars, until Oromë, the Huntsman of the Valar, riding like the wind across the land, discovered by chance the newly awakened Children of Ilúvatar and befriended them. And when Oromë (meaning "Hornblower" in Quenya) returned to the Undying Lands, the Valar held counsel, then summoned the Children to the Kingdom of the Blessed so they might dwell in an eternal realm better suited to the bodies and spirits of the immortal Elves.

In the Great Migration of the Elves Tolkien set out to link the Elves and his idea of their "true tradition" with the history and mythology of the ancient Celts. Oromë the Huntsman is based on a god of the original Celtic Britons. The ancient Welsh knew this god as Arawn the Huntsman, while Tolkien's Grey Elves' name for him was Araw the Huntsman. The Welsh Arawn the Huntsman was from the Otherworld Annwn, but rode often through the forests of the Mortal World. Sometimes identified with the celestial Orion, Arawn befriended the mortal hero Pwyll, the Welsh King of Dyfed. In friendship, they exchanged kingships; so each realm might profit from the wisdom of the other. The Elvish Araw the Huntsman likewise travelled between mortal lands and the immortal realm of Aman.

Tolkien was determined to put the Elves on the right track, in their "true" tradition. Oromë the Great discovered and guided the Elves on the Great Journey into the West through forests, over mountains, and over plains, until at last they reached the shore of Belegaer, the Great Sea of the West. There, Ulmo the Ocean Lord pulled a great island from its roots and carried the Elves over the sea to the Undying Lands. There are Biblical parallels here. Just as the Israelite tribes of Moses in the Old Testament were the Chosen People who fled servitude in Egypt to find their Promised Land, so Tolkien has created a "chosen" race who, by the end of the War of the Ring have all left Middle-earth and journeyed to Eldamar in the Undying Lands. (The complexity, too, of the migrations, genealogies and histories of the various branches of the Elven race of Middle-earth would certainly be a challenge worthy of an Old Testament scholar.)

Grey havens – Welsh singers and Elvish songs

As a child in the rural Midlands, Tolkien became interested in the strange language written on the sides of Welsh coal trucks. He developed an aesthetic sense in language, believing that some languages were "beautiful" and others "ugly". Upon hearing Welsh spoken and, famously, sung in church choirs, Tolkien had no doubt that in Welsh he had discovered one of the world's most beautiful and musical of languages. If Elves had a language, Tolkien believed it was logical to look for its origins in the language of these original Britons. Consequently, he invented an Elven language (Sindar or Grey-Elven) which was based on the structure of the Welsh language.

As Tolkien frequently pointed out himself, the Shire of the Hobbits is analogous for the Shires of the English Midlands on the edge of the Welsh Marches. We have simply to take a quick look at the rough geographic duplication of the coastlines of Wales and Cornwall severed by that distinctive wedge of the Bristol Channel and the Severn River, and walled in by the Welsh Mountains on the Marches of the Shires, for it to become obvious that north and south Lindon are intended to be analogous to Wales and Cornwall.

The history, myths and languages of ancient Wales and Elvish Lindon became two sides of the same coin to Tolkien. The choirs of Wales are renowned throughout the world, while Lindon was the "land of song" – or more precisely, land of "sacred song". Historically, Wales and Cornwall were the last refuges of the true "British" – as distinct from the "English" – people. This distinction between British and English is critical to understanding Middle-earth's cosmology. Tolkien insisted that, properly speaking, the term "British" refers to the Welsh-speaking Celts who settled the land at least two millennia before the arrival of the relatively primitive English (Anglo-Saxon) tribes in the fifth century AD. Through many centuries of contact and government under the Romans, most aristocratic Britons and all the British clergy spoke Latin. Tolkien was well aware of this, and wrote of how the Grey Elf or Sindar language was created to resemble Welsh. Quenya or Elvish Latin was invented to relate to Sindar in a relationship similar to that between Welsh and Latin. Curiously, Tolkien chose Finnish – an obscure language of unknown origin – as the basis for the language of the "Speakers" or "Quendi", the High Elves of Eldamar.

Eldamar: Light Elves and the wise

The High King of the Elves was Ingwë of the Vanyar, the First Kindred of the Elves. Ingwë eventually led his people through the cleft of light to live in the paradise of

Valinor. In this instance, we know exactly what the philological sources for Ingwë and the Vanyar are, as Tolkien once wrote of a Northern heroic warrior named Ingeld, the son of Froda, who was prince of the Heathobards and the enemy of the Shield Danes of Beowulf. Tolkien discovered that behind this tale was a "god the Angles called Ing". This god was one of a race of golden fertility and corn gods, the Vanir. Among the Norsemen, this god is known as Freyr ("the Lord") or Yngvi-freyr ("Ingwë – the Lord"), and so we have the golden-haired Lord Ingwë, the King of the Vanyar and the eponymous first king of Ing-Land (or England).

The King of the Second Kindred was Finwë of the Noldor, Noldor in Quenya meaning "knowledge"; however, we now know from Tolkien's original drafts that the Noldor Elves were originally to be called the "Gnomes". ("Gnome" comes from the Greek "gnosis", meaning "knowledge".) Fortunately, others persuaded Tolkien to revise this. The Noldor were also known as the Wise Elves and the Deep Elves.

Upon the death of his father, King Finwë, Fëanor became High King of the Noldor. Fëanor made the Palantiri spherical crystals known as the "Seeing Stones" that were later given to the Men of Arnor and Gondor. These appear to have been the original prophetic "crystal balls" with which so many fraudulent circus "fortune-tellers" claimed to foretell the future or see into other lands and minds.

As in the Quest of the Holy Grail, Fëanor's quest to recover the Silmarils was to lead to the utter destruction of all of those who pursued it. Like the Grail, the Silmarils had a purity of spirit too great for the mortal world. Similarly, the fiery spirit of Fëanor was finally too great to submit to the rule of the Valar. Feanor led his eight sons and the Noldor into exile in the mortal lands of Middle-earth.

Avalónnë – golden apples of the sun

Avallónë is the port and city of the Teleri Sea Elves on the Lonely Isle named Tol Eressëa. It was from this port that they eventually sailed to the shore of Eldamar in the Undying Lands, (where they would later found the port of Alqualondë). It was from the lamplit quays of Avallónë that the Sea Elves most often sailed to the continent named "Númenor" or "Atalantë" by Tolkien. In Avallónë and Tol Eressëa, Tolkien presents his prototype, or "true myth", of Avallónë which, in later times, was to be thought of as the Earthly Paradise known as Avalon, famous in Arthurian legends. Here came the mortally wounded Arthur who was healed by the nine queens of Avalon and remains there to this day.

Avalon means "Isle of Apples", and it has been claimed that these nine queens are in fact the equivalent of the Muses of Greek mythology. By other accounts, these are the Fortunate Isles known as the Hesperides (or "Westernesse"), where the beautiful daughters of Atlas and Hesperis ("West Wind") tend the tree which bears

Right The great Elvish city of Tirion in Eldamar in the Undying Lands featured a tall tower in which was set a great silver lamp.

the golden apples of immortality. Or could this be the Isle of Idunn, the Norse Goddess of Youth, whose golden apples stopped the gods of Valhalla from being consumed by the ravages of time?

And so we find that the Greeks willingly reveal to us the ancient location of these tales of the "Isle of Apples" and the "Golden Apples of Immortality". For the Isle of the Hesperides actually means "Isle of the Daughters of the West Wind"; the most common translation of the island's name is simply "Westernesse"! And "Westernesse" is the common name for Tol Eressëa, the Isle of the Elves of Avallónë!

As the "Isle of Westernesse" and the "Isle of the Hesperides" are in fact the same places separated only by time and surface appearances, the same may also be true of many of Middle-earth's immortal Elven Queens – they may be discovered in disguise in many a goddess and heroine within the tales of mortal Men. Memories and dreams of the Trees of Light in the Undying Lands, have doubtlessly inspired many stories of an Isle of the Blessed where eternal wealth and eternal life could be won by finding trees on which grew the "Golden Apples of the Sun" and "Silver Apples of the Moon." The real value of such tales of wonder, Tolkien would insist, was that through them, everyday miracles of nature might be made vivid and luminous in our own minds.

Rivendell – Elves and Oxford dons

In a great mountain cleft, there was hidden the realm of Rivendell where stood the House of Master Elrond the Half-Elven, who for 4000 years held open his door to the good and the great of his times. This was especially true for the beleaguered Men of Arnor and Gondor, whom Elrond often took into his home and fostered in times of crisis. Considered the "Last Homely House East of the Sea", Rivendell was a house of wisdom and great learning, and a refuge of kindness for all Elves and Men of goodwill.

Viewing the north-west of Middle-earth as equivalent in latitude to the coastline of Europe and the north shore of the Mediterranean, Tolkien suggests that: "Hobbiton and Rivendell are taken (as intended) to be at about the latitude of Oxford." Tolkien has informed us that The Shire is analogous to rural Warwickshire; Lindon, to Wales and Cornwall. It is quite clear that Rivendell is not just "on the latitude of Oxford", it is an analogy for Oxford as well. Rivendell was an Elvish Oxford, and Oxford during the Great War soon become very like a human Rivendell: a refuge, a house of lore and good counsel in the midst of a world gone mad with slaughter and war. For JRR Tolkien, Oxford was just such a refuge. In fact, that world of slaughter in the Great War nearly consumed Tolkien, as it had consumed almost all of his contemporaries. Ironically, had Tolkien not become violently ill with the debilitating illness known as "trench fever" he probably would not have survived the conflict.

A century before Tolkien's remarks above, the poet Matthew Arnold saw Oxford in the same way: "Oxford, the Oxford of the past, has many faults; and she has paid heavily for them in defeat, in isolation, in want of hold upon the modern world. Yet we in Oxford brought up amidst the beauty and sweetness of that beautiful place, have not failed to seize one truth – the truth that beauty and sweetness are essential characters of a complete human perfection." Matthew Arnold's statement, with a few minor adjustments, could almost be an Elvish manifesto of an eternal creative drive toward perfection.

Rivendell was not only a safe refuge; like Oxford it was a place of learning and long meditation for the world-weary. Rivendell was a house where scribes and scholars might work in peace. In Rivendell, the common tongue was Westron; while the true scholar's choice was the ancient Elvish languages of Sindarin and Quenya. In Oxford, the common tongue was English; while the true scholar's choice was the ancient languages of Latin and Greek. In both of these closed societies, languages were immediate and effective "indicators of social class and distinction". Oxford society, just like Rivendell's, was willfully "out of time" with the contemporary world. However, Master Elrond's use of language was archaic, but not excessively so for someone 6000 years old. Oxford since the early nineteenth century has been, rather magnificently, entitled the "Home of Lost Causes". Rivendell was not without its "last enchantments", but if any place upon Middle-earth is to be awarded the title "Home of Lost Causes" it is without doubt – the-soon-to-be-extinct – "Last Homely House East of the Sea".

Imladris – the Elvish Delphi

There was something else about Rivendell. Something best viewed through examining the word "Imladris", not just its Elvish name, but an alternate reality; something "other", that concerns itself with the Elvish aspects of second sight, prophetic dreams, and waking visions. This House of Lore not only kept historic artefacts and documents; Master Elrond the Half-elven was himself a living history – six millennia of it. In Imladris, Elrond Half-elven was perhaps best consulted as an ancient living oracle.

Tolkien often leaves clues in names: Rivendell's Westron name "Karningul" meaning "Cleft Valley" is repeated in its Sindarin name "Imladris" which means "Deep Cleft Dale" because it is in a hidden rock cleft at the foot of a pass in the Misty Mountains. This location kept Imladris hidden by natural illusions created by the folds in the rock face of the deep-cut valley. This hidden cleft of darkness was also an allusion – in reverse – to a most revealing Cleft of Light in the immortal kingdom of Eldamar. This was the Calacirya, the "Cleft of the Valley of Light", the only pass through the Pelori Mountains which encircle the Undying Lands. This was the Cleft of Light that allowed the Light of the Trees of the Valar to shine out upon Eldamar. The tall, white towers of the kingdom of Tirion – the greatest of all Elven cities – stood in this Valley of Light. This Cleft of Light was the Elvish equivalent to the Doors of Paradise and its light was a divine blessing and inspiration.

In ancient Greece, there was another sacred "Cleft of Light". This was the Oracle at Delphi that was built in a narrow pass through the mountains of Parnassus, sacred to the sun god Apollo. Delphi means "cleft" in Greek. The Oracle of Delphi

Left The tranquil haven of Rivendell gives refuge to the four young Hobbits in their flight from The Shire. In its other-worldly character and role as a seat of Elvish wisdom and lore, Rivendell is the Middle-earth equivalent of the university town of Oxford where JRR Tolkien spent much of his academic career as Professor of Anglo-Saxon.

was the Cleft of Light through which the sacred light of Apollo flowed. That sacred light was of both a literal and a metaphorical nature, for Apollo the sun god was also the god of the intellect, and the god of prophecy. Within the sanctuary of the Temple of Apollo, there was hidden a cleft rock or fissure in the sacred mountain from which rose vapors that induced a trance of prophecy. And as Apollo was also the god of

poets and musicians, there was one more cleft at Delphi. It was the cleft rock or fissure on the side of the sacred mountain that was (and still is) the source of the cool waters of the Castellian Spring that is sacred to Apollo and the Muses and that has the power to inspire poets and musicians.

All the masters of the ancient world came to consult the Oracle at Delphi. The treasures of many cities and the archives of Delphi were protected within this sanctuary by treaty or diplomatic agreement, and to some degree by fear of Apollo's wrath. Like Imladris, Delphi was believed to be under the protection of the river and mountains spirits around it. In *The Lord of the Rings*, an invasion of Imladris is attempted by Ringwraiths, but this was rapidly repelled when the river rose in a mighty flood that swept the demonic horsemen away. Similarly, ancient historians tell of the Persian King Xerxes who, upon invading Greece, ordered his bodyguard to march on the unfortified sanctuary of Delphi. In this attempt, the Persians were utterly destroyed. Their forces were swept away by a thunderous series of flash floods, followed by a massive crush of landslides that blocked the mountain passes and brought an end to the invasion.

The temple of Apollo was the house of record, law and lore. It was also the house of consultation before any great adventure or campaign. Its prophecies were most often double edged, and as such a warning and a caution to the proud and the mighty. The future was not fixed, but determined by personal courage and will. Written across the entrance to Apollo's temple was written "Know thyself". Delphi and Imladris were places where the inner journey was encouraged, before the outer journey was taken in good faith. Delphi and Imladris were both places where fellowships were created and journeys begun. These are refuges from which adventurers set out upon the wide world with hope, and a sign of good fortune.

Mirkwood – perilous forests and enchantresses

Greenwood the Great, was one of the largest ancient forests on Middle-earth. In the Third Age, it became Mirkwood: a place of dread, haunted by invading Orcs, Trolls, Wolves and Werewolves who attacked travellers, while a contamination of Great Spiders infested the Wood. Only the efforts of the Beornings and Woodmen kept even one forest road open through Mirkwood.

Mirkwood is an ancient Anglo-Saxon composite word that conveys a sense of lurking superstitious dread of primeval forests. This convention of Mirkwood – great dark forests filled with evil demonic beings – appears endemic to all ancient and medieval Germanic literature, from mythology to epic poems and romances. Later, elements of hero tales were reduced to mere fairy tales, but the sinister atmosphere of Mirkwood remained. It is certainly found in the fairy tales of the Brother's

Left Although Silvan Elves lived in the north of Mirkwood, by the time of the War of the Ring, this once beautiful forest had largely been consumed by the evil of Sauron. It was home to a colony of Great Spiders, whom Bilbo Baggins encountered during his adventures in *The Hobbit*.

Grimm. The Great Forest is an evil and dangerous place for all in *Little Red Riding Hood*, *Hansel and Gretel*, *Snow White* and *The Sleeping Beauty* – the dark landscape of the Mirkwood is to be found in all these tales. In the heroic age of epic oral poetry, the dark forest was ever present, and always specifically named Mirkwood. In the Norse Ring Saga, Sigurd the Volsung claims the dynastic sword and sets out to slay Tolkien's favourite villain, the evil Fafnir, the "Prince of Dragons". Sigurd enters the darkness of Mirkwood. He stops only to mourn the loss of the "Glittering Heath", now ruined by the corruption of the Serpent. Despite the darkness of Mirkwood, Sigurd follows the great scorched track burned in the earth by the acid slime that seeps from the serpent's scales. This is the poisoned road to the stone chamber of the Dragon. This motif of the contamination of nature is taken up by Tolkien in his cannibal-spider-infested Mirkwood, and the blasted heath and waste land around the lair of his Dragon of Erebor.

Mirkwood has haunted the Gothic imagination and its literature from the earliest times. There may be historic reasons for this. The Anglo-Saxons and their Gothic-German ancestors were ruthless invaders who made their fortunes through the mass murder or enslavement of the indigenous populations of the lands they invaded. These earlier inhabitants – for over two millennia – had been Celts who became outlaws and built refuges deep in the great forests. If any stranger wandered near; the people of the forest had no choice: outsiders had to be killed or taken captive – and never released. For, once discovered, the forest people would themselves all be put to death. Historically, some medieval forests were "haunted" by those who made sure that no one who entered their forests ever returned.

The Celts portrayed the Great Forests very differently: from the inside looking out. The Celts were worshippers of trees and had no fear of forests. The Celts were forest dwellers when they first came to Europe, some 2000 years before the Germanic invaders. They went by night and day into the forests to hunt and gather. They knew and loved the creatures of even the deepest woods. There was no terror in Nature unless it was invoked by the mind of Man. Celtic myths speak of great forests as natural wonders. Wooded valleys and glens were filled with golden light by day; and by night they were filled with moonlight and starlight. In the forests are found miraculous herbs and medicines, as well as nourishing foods. In fact, the forests may provide all the materials needed for life, from the making of clothing to the building of homes. And so it was usually deep in the dense wood, by forest grottoes, wells, or fountains where the Celts worshipped the spirits of wood and water, and found their oracles.

Tolkien's Elves are not solely related to British (or Welsh) Celtic traditions and conventions. Although Tolkien's aesthetics in linguistics condemned Gaelic to

be as "ugly" as Welsh was "beautiful", he discovered much that was wonderful in the ancient myths and legends of Ireland. Tolkien's Elves are not pixies, flower-fairies, gnomes, dwarfs, or goblins of a diminutive and inconsequential kind. They are a powerful, full-blooded people who closely resemble the pre-human Irish race of immortals called the Tuatha Dé Danann. Like the Tuatha Dé Danann, Tolkien's Elves are taller and stronger than mortals, are incapable of suffering sickness, are possessed of greater than human beauty, and are filled with superior wisdom in all things. They ride supernatural horses and understand the languages of animals. They love song, poetry, and music – all of which they compose and perform perfectly.

The remnant of this once mighty Irish race was the Aes Sidhe, or the Sidhe (pronounced "shee"). The name means the "people of the hills", for it was believed that these people withdrew from the mortal realm and hid themselves inside the "hollow hills" or within ancient mounds once sacred to them. In Tolkien, as in Celtic legends, we have remnant populations of these immortals in all manner of hiding places: enchanted woods (such as Lothlórien), hidden valleys (such as Rivendell), in caves (such as Menegroth), in river gorges (such as Nargothrond), and on distant islands (like Avallónë). Tolkien's Elves, like the Sidhe, seldom intrude on the world of men. They are far more concerned with their own affairs and histories.

Above The members of the Fellowship of the Ring enter the Golden Wood of Lothlórien near the stream of Nimrodel. They are soon encountered by Silvan Elves who have seen them from their lookout platforms high in the trees. These platforms are just a minute foretaste of the beautiful tree-city of Caras Galadon at the heart of the forest.

Lothlórien – dream time and desire

In *The Lord of the Rings*, the fairest and most mysterious Elf-kingdom on Middle-earth was hidden within the enchanted forest of the Golden Wood, east of the Misty Mountains. It was called Lothlórien, the "land of blossoms dreaming", and was also known as Lórien ("dreamland") and Laurelindórinan ("valley of the singing gold"). Here the Noldor Queen, Galadriel, and the Sindar King, Celeborn, ruled. "Tall and beautiful, with the hair of deepest gold", Galadriel was robed in white and had great powers of prophecy with her mirror of water.

In the mythology of the ancient Welsh, the most enchanting spirits of the forests were the "White Ladies" which in nearly all ways resemble Galadriel. The White Ladies of the Welsh maintain the traditional affinity of Elves and starlight. All love to walk through the forest beneath the starlit sky. Like Tolkien's Elves, they are also generally perceived by mortals as having eyes like stars, and bodies that shimmer with light. These ancient Celtic forest and water nymphs were guardians of sacred fountains, wells, and grottoes hidden in some deep forest vale.

To reach these refuges it was commonly necessary to pass through or across water that was – as was said of crossing over a river into Lothlórien – "like crossing a bridge in time". They live in a realm outside of time. These White Ladies often lived in incredible crystal palaces beneath water or floating in air, all glowing with silver and golden light. The Arthurian Vivien, the "Lady of the Lake", dressed in white, rose from her palace beneath the lake and presented the sword and scabbard of Excalibur to the rightful king. Water Nymphs with supernatural gifts or weapons have a pedigree older than historical records.

Vivien also raised Lancelot du Lac, before sending him into the world with arms of war. Two thousand years before Vivien, another water nymph armed Achilles for battle in the Trojan War. From the Nixies river nymphs of Siegfried's time to the Nereid sea nymphs of Perseus's time these deities gave protection, prophecies, inspiration, invisibility, and strength to their protégés. In these characteristics we can see Galadriel, who presides over a golden realm of dreams and desires, visions and illusions, gifts and ill-fates.

In ancient Greece, there was a place of healing presided over by the goddess Demeter (very like Galadriel's idol, Yavanna, the Queen of the Earth) at Patrae. This was similar to Galadriel's Mirror, except that this was actually a real mirror which was dipped in a sacred well or pool. Another "mirror" of mythology was the original mirror of Snow White's vain stepmother – the pool of the Muses, known as the "mirror of Aphrodite".

Many of Tolkien's epic romances are presented as the histories of "true myths" which have been reduced to the most basic and obvious of fairy tales. He also particularly liked to demonstrate to his readers how the writers of fairy tales often got their stories wrong. With the case of the Golden Wood of Lothlórien, we see many fairy tale elements of the "Enchanted Forest", "Hidden Kingdom", "Raven-haired Maiden" and "Queen of the Magic Mirror" themes. The Enchanted Forest of Lothlórien contains virtually every element of the story of Snow White (which are explored fully in the section concerning the Dwarves). But as we now see, there are always two beautiful women in the Enchanted Wood: the beautiful dark-haired princess and the wicked queen with the magic mirror. Except, as Tolkien suggests, this is all wrong. The Queen is Snow White's guardian and protector, the Enchanted Forest a place of refuge and healing, the Magic Mirror is a kind of wishing well, and the Enchantress is the embodiment of good fortune.

In *The Lord of the Rings*, the "Snow White" of her time was the Elf, Arwen Undomiel, or "evening maid" who had dark hair and luminous white skin and the voice of a nightingale. Her "prince" is Aragorn, and these long-parted lovers have to overcome many seemingly insurmountable adversities before they can be together. But unlike their fairy-tale counterparts they are not guaranteed to "live happily ever after". In her marriage to a mortal, Arwen is sundered from her people and must sacrifice her immortality.

In *The Silmarillion*, in the First Age, the White Lady with raven hair and ruby lips was the luminous beauty Lúthien. Wherever Lúthien wandered, a clustering trail of snow white niphredils flowered at the touch of her feet. This is almost identical to the Welsh legend from the Mabinogion concerning the raven-haired Olwyn, the most beautiful woman of her age. Olwyn's eyes shone with light, and her skin was white as snow. Olwyn's name means "she of the white tract", so bestowed because "four white trefoils sprang up with her every step on the forest floor."

In the works of Tolkien, the very first of the dark-haired White Ladies is the celestial model for Snow White, Varda, the Queen of the Stars. Varda, the dark-haired Queen of the Night, went by many names including "Fanuilos", which is Sindar for "Snow White".

Above The Oracle of Delphi from ancient Greece, so similar in all but details to the visionary Elvish Queen of Lothlorien, Galadriel.

Left Galadriel and her prophetic Mirror are emblematic of other fairy-tale ladies and their various types of magical mirrors and looking glasses, the most famous being Snow White's wicked stepmother.

Kingdoms of the Dwarves

The door in the mountain

In Tolkien's world, entry into the realm of the Dwarves is made through the secret door-in-the-mountain that cannot be entered except by those who possess its key. In most fairy tales containing the door-in-the-mountain motif, the hero enters a vast subterranean world that is filled with wonder and wealth, peril and wisdom. These tales of magical and forbidding doors-in-the-mountain most often lead to the discovery of a lost inheritance or a cursed hoard of gold, and they require the intelligence of the hero to outwit or pacify the guardians of these treasures within the mountains.

This was certainly true of the Quest to Lonely Mountain, when Thorin and Company sent Bilbo Baggins through a secret mountain door in Tolkien's first novel *The Hobbit*. Occasionally entry to such places is by means of a simple key. More often, however, entry is by means of a spell or through the answering of a riddle, known only to the mountain genius. These vary from the "Open Sesami!" of *Ali Baba and the Forty Thieves*, through the secret spell that opens Aladdin's cave, to the musical tunes which command the stone doors in *The Pied Piper of Hamlyn*.

The greatest of the original Seven Dwarf Kingdoms was Khazad-dûm. In later years, these vast and deep Dwarf mines were known as Moria, and its Great West Door was one of the wonders of Middle-earth. In daylight, not even the smallest crack of the mountain wall could be discerned. By moonlight, however, the great door with its beautiful heraldic symbols and inscriptions glittered with starlit silver when touched by the hand of one who spoke the words of an ancient spell. When the Fellowship of the Ring arrived at the West Door of Moria, it was sealed, but, as Gandalf states: "these doors are probably governed by words". Only Gandalf's great knowledge of ancient languages allowed him to answer the riddle and speak the word "mellon", meaning "friend".

In Tolkien's Middle-earth, entry into the secret world of the Dwarves had to be achieved through language. Creatively speaking, for Tolkien, words were the keys to all the lost kingdoms of Middle-earth, a world discovered through languages, runes, gnomic script, and riddles. These are the means used to unlock the doors of imagination. Tolkien started with the word "Dwarf". It was a very ancient word, at least four millennia old. It seems to have its origin in the Indo-European root word "dhwergwhos", meaning something "tiny". To begin with, Tolkien insisted the plural must be "Dwarves", not "Dwarfs". Tolkien wanted specifically to address the issue of the Dwarf as a member of a race of bearded, stunted people who lived in caverns beneath the mountains, not simply as a human of diminished size. He began his attempt to define and standardize the race by recognizing a proper plural term for these people. Tolkien came up with "Dwarves", although he acknowledged that, in proper linguistic terms, it would be more correct to call them "Dwarrows".

Norse sagas and fairy tales

Through Indo-European root words in the earliest Germanic writing of ancient Goth and Lombard (or Langobard – "Long Beard") texts, JRR Tolkien concluded that there was a widespread belief in dwarfs as a powerful but stunted subterranean race of demons or spirits who lived within mountains. These dwarfs were also guardians of treasures and magical gifts, considered masters of fire and forge, and the makers of weapons and jewels. In Middle-earth, we find Tolkien remains consistent with that ancient tradition: his Dwarves are the genii of the mountains, just as Hobbits are the genii of tilled soil and farmlands, and Ents are the genii of the forests. Through his

Left Ali Baba hides in a tree and thus overhears the password used by the Forty Thieves in order to enter a cave full of treasure. A popular motif in many fables and stories, Tolkien too has the Fellowship of the Ring enter a hidden door into the Mines of Moria through Gandalf's utterance of a secret password.

Above As with the dwarfs of many other mythological traditions, Tolkien's Dwarves are ferocious in battle, as Thorin Oakenshield and his army demonstrated in The Battle of the Five Armies.

research, Tolkien felt that he was able to understand fully the true nature and character of this secretive, stunted, mountain-dwelling race. He concluded that his Dwarves were exactly comparable to the Norsemen of Scandinavia, that proud race of warriors, craftsmen, and traders who were so vividly portrayed in the Icelandic Sagas – similar in all but the Norsemen's love of the sea.

The Dwarves of Middle-earth were probably most like the ancient Germanic forebears of the Vikings before they encountered ships or horses. Both were stoic and independent in nature. They were alike in their admiration of strength and bravery, in their sense of honour and loyalty, and in their love of gold and treasure. They were all but identical in their skill in the wielding and forging of weapons, in their stubborn pride, and in their relentless will to avenge any perceived injustice.

Like the Norsemen, Dwarves are brave and fearless on their own ground, but distrustful and dismissive of all that they do not know. Unlike the warrior culture of the Scandinavian Norsemen, who were also sea rovers, foresters, and farmers, Tolkien's Dwarves are actually fearful of the open sea, the deep forest, and the wide plain. They would rather carry a horse than ride it, cut down a tree than climb it, or burn a boat than sail it. Dwarves only find security in the deep roots of mountains and joy in the working of gold and precious metals, the forging of weapons of steel, the carving of stone, and the setting of gems.

From traditional fairy tales concerning dwarfs, Tolkien also attempted to discover more of this archetypal race: the connection with the mines, the hoarding of treasure, the forging of supernatural weapons, and the creation of gifts with magical qualities. From the examination of tales such as *Rumpelstiltskin*, Tolkien came to believe that his Dwarves must have secret names, a love of riddles, and a secret language written in runes. Tolkien decided that, although Dwarves were not exclusively male, their women (and also their children) were few and so hidden away that they were never seen by other peoples. Also, many of the Dwarves' greatest passions were reserved for the acquiring and shaping of gold and other such materials of the earth. In *Rumpelstiltskin*, Tolkien also observed the essential association of dwarfs with magic rings of power. That fairy story, with its motif about spinning pure gold from straw, offers a direct link from the dwarfs to the great epic ring quests of the German *Nibelungenlied* and the Norse *Volsunga Saga*. Rumpelstilskin's spinning wheel is a fairy-tale version of the magical powers embodied in the dwarf-forged ring of these ancient myths. This magical gold ring was known as "Andvarinaut" in the *Nibelungenlied*, meaning "the ring of Andvari the Dwarf". It was also called "Andvari's Loom" because of its power to reproduce itself eternally. It was the ultimate source of the cursed gold of the Nibelung and Volsung treasures.

In Norse myth, this ring comes into the possession of Odin. It is called "Draupnir", the "Dripper", because every nine days it dripped eight new gold rings. Here we see again the significance of the number nine: the number of the sorcerer. As king of the Norse gods, Odin was truly the Lord of the Rings. Draupnir was the One Ring that was the symbol of his dominion over the Nine Worlds of Norse cosmology, just as Sauron's One Ring was of his dominion over Middle-earth.

The Seven Sleepers

Two of the major influences on Tolkien's Dwarves were the fairy tale *Snow White and the Seven Dwarfs* and an Icelandic poem, the *Voluspa* (meaning "Sybil's Prophecy"), a powerful seeress's vision of the creation, evolution, and ultimate destruction of the Norse cosmos. From the *Voluspa*, Tolkien discovers the name "Durin", a shadowy and mysterious creator of the dwarfs. It must surely have provoked him to note that the creator who "awakens" a race has a name which means "sleeper". "Durin" can also accurately be translated as "Sleepy", as it was when adopted (from the same source) in the fairy tale of Snow White's Seven Dwarfs.

Typically, Tolkien believed the fairy tale had actually scrambled the original myth or history of the ancient race. In the beginning, Tolkien decided, it was the

Below The dwarf king Thorin, whose name Tolkien drew from the Norse Roll of Dwarves.

Seven Dwarfs who were the "sleepers", not Snow White. In this fairy tale, what he saw was a jumbled account of the origin of the dwarf race. The Seven Dwarfs may have been the first of their race, but Durin the Sleeper was not their maker. Tolkien came to the conclusion that Durin was the first of the "Seven Sleepers" – the ancestral fathers of the race – who rested in deep caverns "beneath stone" until the time came when they might "awaken" to fulfil their destiny.

The origins of this idea, the legends of dynastic ancestors "sleeping" in caverns beneath mountains, is one that is common to many nations. King Arthur, Charlemagne, and Ghengis Khan are just a few of the national heroes reputed to have slept beneath mountains while waiting to be called to the defence of their country in its hour of greatest need. The story of Rip Van Winkle is an American version of this legend. In order to find exactly seven sleepers beneath the mountain in mythology, however, we must go further afield, to the mystical legends of Islam and India. Here the seven sleepers are variously the seven sages, seven prophets, or the ancestors of the seven kings of seven kingdoms.

Mountain gods and masters of fire

Once Tolkien had discovered his Seven Sleepers, he found himself thinking about their maker. In the beginning, Tolkien tells us, the Seven Fathers of the Dwarves were conceived and shaped by Aulë the Maker of Mountains, Master of Fire, Smith of the Valar. It was he, whom the Dwarves knew as "Mahal", who fashioned the race from the substances of the deep earth. From Aulë came the desire to search down into the roots of mountains, a search to discover the brightest of metals and the most beautiful jewels of the earth. With the disocvery of these raw materials came the desire to master such crafts as the carving of stone, forging of metal, and cutting of gems. In Aulë the Maker of Mountains and Smith of the Valar, what we discover is a being who most resembles that of the ancient Greek god of fire, Hephaestus (the Roman god Vulcan), who was also the smith of the Olympian gods. Like Hephaestus, Aulë was true to the spirit of the pure craftsman and artisan, someone who created for the joy of the making, not for possession or for its use in gaining power and dominion over others.

It seems, however, that the Dwarves often strayed from the true and ideal nature of their Maker, and in such circumstances tragedy often befell them. It must be said that, in their skills and passion for war, and in their wrathful and violent nature, the Dwarves often appeared to have more in common with another group – the warrior cult of Thor. Unlike the smith of the gods, Thor, the Norse god of thunder, found glory in battle and honour in the hoarding of gold won in battle by virtue of his war hammer, the Dwarf-forged thunderbolt.

In their conception, Aulë's Seven Fathers of the Dwarves were in many ways similar to the creatures conceived by the smith god of the Greeks, Hephaestus. These appeared to be living creatures, but in fact were robot-like automatons who were designed to help him in his smithy to beat metal and work the forges. The original Seven Fathers of the Dwarves were in the beginning like those automatons: incapable of independent thought or life. They could only move on command or by the thought of their master. It was Ilúvatar who gave them the gift of true life. Yet Ilúvatar would not permit the Dwarves to walk upon Middle-earth before the awakening of his own creations, the Elves. Hence the Seven Fathers of the Dwarves slept through the ages until the eternally dark skies were filled with starlight by Varda, the Star Queen.

There can be little doubt of Tolkien's intentions here, for one of the many names for the Star Queen is the High Elvish "Fanuilos", which simply translated is "Snow White". This is somewhat disorienting. Having just got used to the revelation that the "Seven Dwarves" were the real "sleepers" in the "true" tradition of the fairy tale, we now discover that it is Snow White – the supposed "Sleeping Beauty" – who is actually responsible for awakening the Seven Fathers of the Dwarves.

Salvation of the Dwarves

Dwarves find that all sentient beings in a forest harbour hostility towards them. On an elemental level, the essence of this hostility may also be seen as the ancient feud between mountain and forest. The elements of stone, iron, and fire are in conflict with those of earth, wood, and water. The genius of the mountain seems continually to be at war with the genius of the forest.

Initially wary of the Enchantress of the Golden Wood, Gimli the Dwarf experiences a sudden conversion in sentiment towards Queen Galadriel that is almost religious in its nature and intensity. Gimli asks the Queen for a golden lock hair instead of a gift of precious metal. Gimli's request conjures up the strange figure of Rumpelstiltskin once again. The "nasty dwarf" returns, but is now transformed into a "gallant dwarf". The Dwarf's heirloom is three golden hairs set in crystal. His heritage is a dreadful pun: "hair-loom". (Here again the word play in Sindarin: mellon = friend, mel = love, and also mel = gold.) Gimli the Dwarf has discovered that the "true gold" of his desire is that of love and friendship.

Snow White and the mirror of Galadriel

There was one other beauty of royal blood in the Golden Wood, the Princess of the Elves, Arwen Evenstar, whose dark beauty rivalled that of the golden Galadriel under whose protection she remained. Arwen's beauty was renowned and most akin to Varda, the Queen of the Stars. Varda was celebrated by the Dwarves, for in the Rekindling of the Stars she created the Seven Stars known to the Dwarves as Durin's Crown, which brought about the Awakening of the Seven Fathers of the Dwarves. And it was Varda who, for her own brilliance, was named "Fanuilos", meaning "Snow White". So great was the beauty of Arwen, the future Queen of the Dúnedain, that she was believed to be the Star Queen come down to Middle-earth. Other than that, Arwen Evenstar was another manifestation of the original Snow White.

Beyond what we have already considered about the legend of Snow White and the Elves, there can be little doubt of a deeply buried theme within *The Lord of the Rings*. Simply describing the circumstances of the two Elf Queens in the Golden Woods easily reproduces the plot of Snow White, and suggests where the fairy-tale writers went wrong. Let us consider: a beautiful dark-haired, pale princess is hidden away in an enchanted wood ringed against entry by bewildering powers and an invisible army of deadly archers. In this hidden kingdom, the princess is carefully hidden away from the world. She is constantly watched over by a beautiful, immortal enchantress who casts mighty spells, repels suitors, and consults a magic mirror. It all sounds rather familiarly like Snow White variations. Particularly when we bring in earlier variations on The Sleeping Beauty, and the Seven Fathers of the Dwarves.

The Magic Mirror of Galadriel seems to have one element (hard to identify at first) which would place the matter beyond dispute. It is something to do with the supposed motive for the enchantress who is constantly gazing in her magic mirror. Tolkien suggests, of course, that there is no rivalry and that the enchantress is simply protecting her adoptive daughter. The fairy tale, however, settles for the vanity of the wicked stepmother and her jealousy of her stepdaughter's beauty.

Left Moria, or Khazad-dûm, was once the greatest of all Dwarf kingdoms. It was the ancestral home of Durin, the first of the Seven Fathers of the Dwarves of Middle-earth.

Tolkien makes one very obvious nod to this tradition in the fairy tale, in the running debate between Éomer, King of Rohan, and Gimli the Dwarf over the relative beauty of Queen Arwen of Gondor and Galadriel of Lothlórien. Although the two Queens in Tolkien are far too virtuous to have any part in this rivalry, it is placed there specifically as a nod to the fairy tale. And it is easy to see how some mischievous teller of fairy tales might invent an evil enchantress who is filled with hatred at the beauty of Snow White and asks her magic mirror: "Who is the fairest of them all?"

Gimli's glittering kingdom

All the Dwarves in Tolkien are named in the Norse Roll of the Dwarves, except for one. That one is Gimli. It is a name mentioned in one other ancient Norse text. That text is the *Voluspa*, or "Sybil's Prophecy". Gimli, however, is not the name of a

Below The Glittering Caves of Aglarond eventually become the dominion of the dwarf Gimli, one of the heroes of *The Lord of the Rings*. Gimli's name means "glittering" and is taken from the name of the refuge created for the survivors of the Battle of Ragnarok (which marked the end of the world) in Norse legend.

warrior, but rather a place. It is a place of salvation after the great battle of Ragnarok and the destruction of the World. Meaning "glittering", Gimli is a newborn paradise for the Norse people. After the War of the Ring, many of the Dwarves of Middle-earth are invited by Gimli to a new Kingdom-under-Mountain where are found the wondrous caverns of Helm's Deep. Gimli was celebrated as the Lord of Aglarond, a name meaning the "Glittering Caves".

The telling of the history of the Dwarves was very much from the views of Elves and Men. A Dwarf chronicle might well perceive events of this time from a very different perspective. Indeed, if Dwarves recorded the events of these times, three acts of not immediately obvious significance which were achieved by Gimli, son of Glóin, would likely be considered the most important outcome of the conflict: Gimli's journey through the Golden Wood of Lothlórien, the discovery of the Glittering Caves of Aglarond, and Gimli's departure over the Western Sea.

By these three acts, Gimli became for the Dwarves what Eärendil the Mariner was to Elves and Men: the redemption and salvation of his people. In the Golden Wood, Gimli gained absolution for ancient transgressions and forgiveness for an evil that had brought dishonour upon the Dwarves. In the Glittering Caves, Gimli rediscovered the true calling of his people and, in fulfilment of a prophecy, discovered his fate. In sailing across the Western Sea, Gimli – alone of his race – was allowed to enter the Undying Lands and may even have been granted an audience with Mahal, or Aulë, the Maker of Mountains. If this be so, then of Gimli it can truthfully be said, "He has gone to meet his Maker".

Domain of the Ents

Shepherds of trees

JRR Tolkien was an unashamed worshipper of trees. From childhood, he had admired and loved these ancient life forms and believed that they were in some way sentient beings. Once asked about the origin of his Ents, Tolkien wrote: "I should say that Ents are composed of philology, literature and life. They owe their name to the 'eald enta geweorc' of Anglo-Saxon." The Anglo-Saxon reference is to a fragment of a hauntingly beautiful Old English poem, *The Wanderer*. The word "enta" was usually translated as "giant", and the phrase related to the prehistoric stone ruins, considered to be the work of an ancient lost race of giants. However, beyond Ent being an Anglo-Saxon name for "giant", the inspiration for Tolkien's March of the Ents came about in a rather negative way. This was through his almost heretical dislike and, indeed, disapproval of William Shakespeare's treatment of myths and legends. His greatest abuse was heaped upon one of the playwright's most popular plays, *Macbeth*.

The creation of the Ents, Tolkien once explained, "is due, I think, to my bitter disappointment and disgust from schooldays with the shabby use made in Shakespeare of the coming of 'Great Birnam wood to high Dunsinane hill': I longed to devise a setting in which the trees might really march to war." Once again, Tolkien believed that he had written a story true to this tradition. He felt Shakespeare had trivialized and misinterpreted an authentic myth, providing a cheap, simplistic interpretation of the prophecy of this march of the wood upon the hill. Perhaps too much should not be read into this; Tolkien, sometimes amused, sometimes irritated by those who looked for sources and hidden meanings in his work, was quite capable of putting up a false scent on occasion. But certainly, in his own March of the Ents, the fundamental opposition of spirits of forest and mountain was revealed and portrayed in a way which lends power and dignity to the miracle of a "wood" marching on the "hill".

On a level of personal amusement, the Ents were also meant to gently satirise Oxford dons and particularly hidebound philologists (among whom Tolkien would number himself). Ents, like academics, were long on the discussion of problems, but slow to take action. Often, however, action proved unnecessary – in both Oxford and the Entwood – as the debates outlasted the problems. A discussion in Entish, however, must have been a philology student's nightmare. It was slow beyond human endurance because each thing named must include the whole history of the thing: "leaf to root", as Ents might say. Consequently, Ent gatherings, or "moots" – with

Right Treebeard the Ent was an affectionate parody of Tolkien's friend and fellow fantasy writer, CS Lewis. The propensity of Tolkien's circle of friends, "The Inklings", for loquaciousness on the origins of words was reflected in the Entmoot in which the Ents discuss at great length what, if any action they will take against the treacherous wizard Saruman.

their qualifications, additions, exceptions, and verbal footnotes on every point – must have had a special savour for those who were familiar with the editorial meetings of the *Oxford English Dictionary* compilers. Treeebeard is a "Tree of Lore", and one might argue that Tolkien's narrative of the story of Treebeard and the Entwood in *The Lord of the Rings* amounts exactly to Treebeard's full name. During the last decades of his life, Tolkien acknowledged in an interview that the leader of the Ents was specifically meant as a good-humoured lampooning of his friend and colleague, CS Lewis, the author of *The Chronicles of Narnia*, complete with his booming voice, his absurd "Hrum, Hroom" interjections, and the authority of a complete know-it-all – who, irritatingly, usually did know it all.

To find beings of myth who do correspond directly to the Ents, Tolkien only had to look back into local English folklore, where the Green Man plays a distinctive part. He is most often seen simply as a face, enlaced in the stonework of a church porch, or in the carved woodwork of its interior. Foliage curls around and sprouts from his ears, nostrils, mouth: even his eyes. Green Man stories and carvings were common in the west Midlands and the Welsh Marches just beyond. He was a Celtic nature spirit, probably linked to a spring-time fertility cult, in which he represented the coming of the new growth in victory over the powers of ice and frost. Essentially benevolent, he could also be over-powerful and destructive, like the Green Knight overcome by Sir Gawain in the Middle English poem *Sir Gawain and the Green Knight*.

The Green Man theme is elaborated in a celebrated book which Tolkien had certainly read, Sir James Frazer's *The Golden Bough*, first published in 1922. Frazer showed that many cultures believed trees to be inherently worshipful, or to be tenanted by spirits. But it goes beyond that. "The conception of trees and plants as animated beings naturally results in treating them as male and female, who can be married to each other in a real, and not just a figurative sense." Having foreshadowed the Ents' tragic loss of their wives, Frazer also gives evidence for the Ents' affinity with water. "I shall show, first," he wrote, "that trees considered as animate beings are credited with the power of making the rain to fall, the sun to shine, flocks and herds to multiply, and women to bring forth easily; and, second, that the very same powers are attributed to tree-gods conceived as anthropomorphic [human-like] beings or as actually incarnate in living men.

The semi-sentient Huorns, who inspire such terror in Saruman's Orc army, represent the wilder, more dangerous aspect of the Green Man: an inhuman power tapping the deepest sources of the natural world. Frazer records cases where fowls, animals, even children, were sacrificed to placate the demonic spirit of certain trees.

Such anthropological lore was of course just the basic raw material from which JRR Tolkien fashioned a mythology which was timeless, rooted in human

experience, and yet wholly his own. No wonder he felt Shakespeare's moving wood in *Macbeth*, in which the soldiers simply hacked off a branch to bear in front of them, to be a slight and trivial thing compared with the profound potential and many attributes of the ancient and venerated spirits of the forest.

The march of the Ents and Huorns

In Act V, scene v of Shakespeare's *Macbeth*, the doomed Scottish king is readying himself for battle. A messenger enters and tells him, "As I did stand my watch upon the hill,/I looked toward Birnam, and anon methought/The wood began to move/... Within this three mile may you see it coming./ I say, a moving grove." This impression of movement however, was simply created by the advance of Macbeth's enemies through the trees. Tolkien had something far more ambitious in mind, and has his Ents rouse up the spirits of the forest, so that it is the trees themselves that really do march towards the citadel of their enemy, Saruman, who has been using the trees to fuel his evil furnaces.

The appearance of the Huorns, the demonic tree spirits under the guidance of the Ents, brought real terror to their foes. The Huorns may have been Ents who in time had grown treeish, or perhaps trees that had grown Entish, but they were certainly wrathful, dangerous, and merciless. In the Huorns, we have a dramatization of an avenging army of "Green Men" (like Gawain's Green Knight) making an attack on all evil creatures who are hostile to the spirits of forests.

Left The March of the Ents, after which the Ents and Huorns destroy Saruman's citadel at Isengard, gave Tolkien the opportunity to develop the idea of a forest coming to life, which he thought had been so poorly achieved by none less than the Bard himself, William Shakespeare, in his play *Macbeth*.

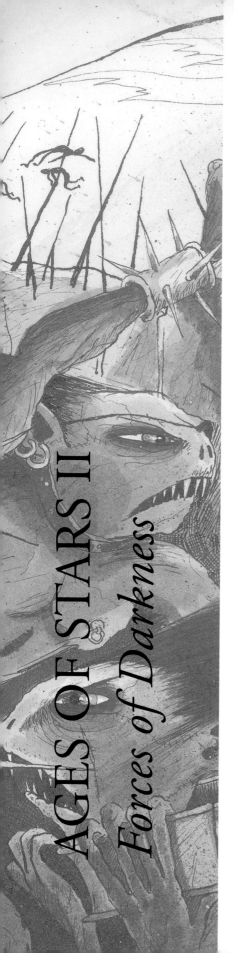

Legions of Orcs

Fairy-tale goblins

"Once there was a Goblin living in a hole." So begins a little song in a story that JRR Tolkien read as a child. It quite obviously resonated in his mind because, several decades later, Tolkien was to write about another diminutive, hole-dwelling creature in his first novel, which began with the famous first line: "In a hole in the ground there lived a hobbit."

The story which provided Tolkien with this inspiration is *The Princess and the Goblin*, by George MacDonald. Published in 1872, it is largely concerned with conflicts between diminutive miners and goblins in underground tunnels, which strongly foreshadowed the subterranean skirmishes between Tolkien's Hobbits and Goblins.

In Tolkien's world, however, the real conflict is between Goblins and another diminutive race, the Dwarves – who are miners as well. Dwarves make dangerously persistent enemies, as proved by the seven year War of the Dwarves and the Orcs that took place towards the end of the Third Age of the Sun. It is a conflict with echoes in various mining cultures, from Cornwall to China, where goblins or demons have been said to sabotage miners in tunnels, hindering their work out of sheer malice and spite.

In Tolkien's story, oversized Hobbit feet are important. In MacDonald's story, oversized goblin feet are important – but for different reasons. Tolkien's Hobbit feet are seen as a strong and positive characteristic. MacDonald's goblin feet are their only weakness, as the miners defeat the Goblins by stamping on their feet and singing magic spells. Tolkien once commented that he never could believe in goblins with soft feet. In Tolkien's story, Goblins could be repelled by certain spells, but their feet were iron-shod; it was the Hobbits who went barefoot. Hobbits and Goblins appear to have been preoccupied with feet.

In MacDonald's story, however, we have the rhyme: "Once there was a goblin living in a hole: busy he was cobblin' a shoe without a sole." This rhyme is a kind of riddle – and one worthy of a Hobbit at that: why does the goblin make a shoe without a sole? Because the goblin is a creature without a soul! Tolkien's Goblins may be protected by iron-shod shoes, but they share MacDonald's goblins' soulless condition; Tolkien's barefoot Hobbits, too, share the same soulless condition (since none of the non-human inhabitants of Middle-earth have a soul).

In Tolkien's novels, the Hobbit and the Goblin are two diminutive, hole-dwelling races that embody the struggle between the forces of good and evil.

Creatively, the Hobbit and Goblin seem to have emerged from the same "hole" in Tolkien's imagination, but with opposite natures. It is only in the tale of *The Hobbit*, however, that the terms "Hobgoblins" and "Goblin" are used. When it came to the writing of *The Lord of the Rings* and *The Silmarillion*, Tolkien decided that he would employ a more seriously evil name for these creatures: the Orc. And as we would come to expect from Tolkien, this choice of name was not without its own meaningful reasons.

The origins of the Orcs

Orcs are the evil demons known in Anglo-Saxon texts as the "Ornacea", meaning "walking corpse", the living dead motivated by envy and enslaved by the Lord of the Rings. It is also a name with links to *Beowulf*'s Orcneas, or demon spirits, and to the Latin "orcus", meaning "hell". In turn, later Latin and Greek writers of natural history gave the name "Orc" or "Orcus" to the real-life monster of the deep, the black-and-white killer whale, and *Orcus* remains the scientific name for the killer whale today.

Above Tolkien's Orcs are not "born", rather created from the tortured forms of Elves. With this idea, Tolkien echoes the Christian concept that Satan could not create new life – of which only God is capable – rather, he can only corrupt existing life forms into leading a life in the service of evil.

Tolkien's Orcs originated in the Pits of Utumno in the First Age of Stars, when Melkor captured many of the newly risen race of Elves and took them to his dungeons where he tortured and transformed them into a Goblin race of slaves who were as loathsome as Elves were fair. They were hideous, stunted, and muscular, with yellow fangs, blackened faces and red slits for eyes.

In a letter to fans, Tolkien wrote "… since in my myth at any rate I do not conceive of the making of souls or spirits, things of an equal order if not an equal power to the Valar, as a possible 'delegation', I have represented at least the Orcs as pre-existing real beings on whom the Dark Lord has exerted the fullness of his power in remodeling and corrupting them, not making them…"

This is an important point because Tolkien's system of thought did not countenance the possibility of evil being able to create something on its own. Therefore Melkor had to corrupt other spirits and creatures. This he did in great variety. Some spirits he corrupted, like Sauron, were great; others, like the Orcs, were not. Most of them plainly (and biologically) were a corruption of Elves (and probably later also of Men). Always, however, among them (as special servants and spies of Melkor, and as leaders) there must have been numerous corrupted minor spirits who assumed similar bodily shapes.

Below The emnity between Orcs and Dwarves went far back into the history of Middle-earth. Here we see Azog, the Orc leader, during the Battle of Azanulbizar which takes place during the War of the Orcs and Dwarves, outside the East Gate of Moria.

Orcs had about as much independence as have, say, domestic dogs or horses of their human masters. Those whose business it was to direct them often took Orkish shapes, although they were greater and more terrible. Thus it was that the histories speak of Great Orcs or Orc-captains who were not slain and who reappeared in battle over numbers of years far longer than the span of the lives of Men.

In time, it also became clear that Men could, under the domination of Melkor or his agents, be reduced almost to an Orkish level of mind or habits in just a few generations; they then would mate, or could be made to mate, with Orcs, producing new breeds, often larger and more cunning. There is no doubt that long afterwards, in the Third Age, Saruman the White discovered this, or learned of it through lore, and in his lust for mastery committed this, his wickedest deed: the interbreeding of Orcs and Men.

The blackness of Orcs

One of the meanings of "orc", noted in the Oxford English Dictionary, is derived from the Latin word "orcus", found occasionally in 16th century English as "orc", meaning a devouring monster. The Orcs in the Tolkien tales provide a counterbalance to the Elves, in every way. The Elves are fair, the Orcs are hideous. They are also black, and this has caused some distress to readers who have seen in it a slur on black-skinned humans. While JRR Tolkien was by no means a politically-correct writer or thinker, it is unfair to impute racism towards him. The Orcs are not human. The opposition of Black and White is a basic motif of *The Lord of the Rings*, expressed in a great variety of ways, most notably perhaps in the emergence of the reincarnated wizard Gandalf as Gandalf the White, the great opponent of the Dark Lord. But this counterpointing is not in the least way a purpose or motive of the story, in the sense of making a statement like "Black = Bad, White = Good." We should perhaps remember the hideous pallor of the creature Gollum. Tolkien, writing in the mid-twentieth century, was using a convention which was commonplace in English and European thought for centuries before him, and which has only in recent years become a controversial and deservedly sensitive issue.

Their function within the wider creative scheme of the tales is to contribute towards the "balance of evil": to show what the effects of Melkor's and Sauron's fatal pride could be in establishing a pattern of evil-doing that had ever-widening and more disastrous repercussions. On a more straightforward narrative level, they provide the necessary, innumerable and terrifying army of the Enemy, confronted by the far less numerous forces of Good. All Tolkien's descriptions of the Orcs create a sense of vast, anonymous numbers: they are like a swarm, a devastating wave. They come pouring from their warren-holes with impersonal, insect-like inexorability, often compared by

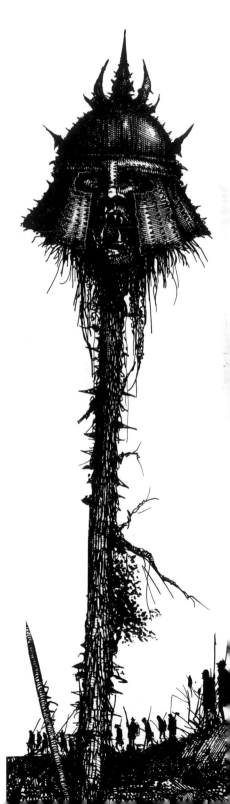

the author to flies or ants. In battle they have a mindless strength and commitment; but also a dangerous weakness; if something should shake that ferocious concentration, then the whole mass would be arrested, uncertain, suddenly vulnerable. Elves, men, dwarves, think on their feet, but the orcs can only follow orders.

Orcs and demons of mythology

The concept and nature of Orcs, evil underlings mindlessly doing the bidding of their evil master, have resonance with numerous myths and tales from around the world. The most obvious starting point, perhaps, is the Bible. For Dionysus, the Areopagite, demons were angels who had rebelled against God and fallen. Their leader was Satan. Before his fall, Satan was known as Lucifer, meaning "bearer of light". He was very powerful, clever, beautiful (the beauty of the devil), arrogant, seductive, wily, a rebel against any law, treacherous, and perverse. He was the "prince of the world" and was below, while the gods were on high.

In this Old Testament world, demons were invisible and innumerable. Each person had a thousand to his right and ten thousand to his left. They preferred to live in isolated, unclean places such as deserts and ruins, and they were to be greatly feared, especially at night. They attacked animals and men, and were the cause of physical ailments and mental problems. They also provoked wild passions and rage, and caused jealousy.

There are, however, earlier incarnations of evil than in the stories of the Bible. In ancient Persia, the kingdom of Bactria where Iran is today, the prophet Zoroastra lived in the second half of the seventh century and the first half of the sixth century BC. In his teachings, his character Angra Mainyu was a prototype for the Christian devil. Angra Mainyu was a foul spirit; he belonged to death, filth, and rottenness, and inspired disgust. As a sign of contempt, in many texts his name was written back to front with vile descriptions. They even went so far as to say that he did not exist and never would. The forces he took – those of the lizard, the serpent, and the fly – were only lent to him for a time and were to disappear like evil. Evil was the opposite of existence. Angra Mainyu, who started off as the equal of Ahura Mazda, the Wise Lord, ended up by gradually disappearing.

And just as Melkor had his Orcs, so Angra Mainyu had his *daevas*. They caused plagues and diseases, and fought against every form of religion. Originally classified as spirits, these creatures became downgraded to demons. The word "devil" is derived from their name. The daevas were controlled by seven archdemons, out of which the most powerful was Aka Manah, or "Evil Mind". Among the other archdemons was Azi Dahaka, or "Fiendish Snake" – in a similar way to Tolkien's Orcs, he was part demon, part human.

Earlier still is the civilization of Mesopotamia, the land between the Euphrates and the Tigris in modern-day Iraq. Among the tales of these Sumerian peoples, and the subsequent kingdoms of Assyria and Babylon, there is the character of Erra, the "Lord who prowls by night". Erra is the cruel, unforgiving god of the underworld – a hunter god, a god of plague, a god of war. He has the power to open the door to the underworld, to allow the passage of a soul. His underlings were the Sebitti, vicious warriors who killed both people and animals at his command. Erra would rally them whenever he felt the urge for war.

In one story, Erra worked out a vast plan for death and bloodshed. He wanted to destabilize the world, which was living in excess, overturning its customs, destroying its foundations, killing the majority, and disturbing the order of the gods. Marduk, under whose rule the excess had occurred, objected by saying that he had already killed many of his people through the Great Flood and would not do so again. Erra was insistent, however, answering all Marduk's objections and promising that he would soundly maintain the delicate balance between heaven and earth, and would make sure that the temple was guarded by the gods Anu and Enlil. He also swore that nothing would change and that all would live in peace and prosperity.

And then Erra broke out. The temples were profaned, inhabited places became deserts, rogues had access to the palaces of princes, sons hated their fathers and mothers hated their daughters, lame men ran faster than normal ones, young people were buried by the old, and man ate man. All values were turned upside down, and no one could escape death.

Orcs of other cultures

Orcs share many similarities with mythical creatures from around the world. In Chinese tales, the equivalent are the repulsive creatures known as the "kouei". They were very large, with a black or green face and long, sharpened teeth. Their faces were covered with long hair. The kouei wandered in corrupt places and through filth, transforming themselves into water demons and making their way into men's lungs so that they could introduce harmful and even lethal substances.

Illness, accidents, and catastrophes were all the doing of the kouei, but they could be pacified by exorcisms and sacrifices. They were, however, rarely sympathetic to humans and were the incarnation of "p'o", the evil spirits which surrounded corpses when they had been freed of their transcended souls. They were often identified with the spirits of the dead, especially those who had died by accident or were murdered.

In Indian Hindu mythology, it was the "Raksha" who were evil spirits representing every hostile force. They appeared either in horrible guises or in a very beguiling form. It was said that they entered abandoned corpses, ate the flesh, and

Above The Pits of Utumno were the site of the creation of the race of Orcs by Melkor, during the First Age of Stars.

Left In an attempt to overwhelm his enemies in the War of the Ring, Sauron made a race of "super" Orcs, the Uruk-hai, who shared many characteristics with the demons of Indian and Persian myths.

then made them obey their will, in order to spread evil all around them. The Raksha's leader was Ravana, the enemy of Rama. He was the head of a kingdom which was always in conflict with the gods and the work of the devout.

In Japan, the "tenga" were closely bound to the mountains, appearing suddenly and bewitching humans. They possessed magic powers, changed their appearance, stole, and could make themselves invisible. Their actions were generally malicious – kidnapping children, sowing discord, making buildings crumble, disrupting religious ceremonies, and even setting fire to temples. They were usually represented as birds with powerful claws.

Below Saruman sent an army of Orcs and Uruk-hai against the forces defending the fortress of Helm's Deep. Although the Orcs were successful in breaching the defences, they were ultimately destroyed by timely reinforcements of Rohirrim warriors and the giant Huorns.

In Haiti and Latin America, there were brotherhoods of particularly evil sorcerers who met in secret places. They held great feasts there to celebrate their crimes and performed rites designed to take away the souls of their enemies so that they could have complete mastery over them. It was said that "they had consumed them". Those enemies became, through their magic rites, what were known as "zombies", the living dead. They were total automatons, under the orders of those who had consumed them. They vomited without hesitation or scruple, and committed crimes and atrocities that had been dictated to them, thus enabling those who were really responsible to escape punishment.

Troll Tribes

Giants, Ents, and Olog-hai

Trolls were a menace to any travellers who ventured out by night on the lonely roads, forest trails, and mountain passes of Middle-earth. They were twice the height and bulk of the largest humans, and had a skin of green scales like flint armour. Trolls were rock hard and powerful, yet, in the sorcery of their making, there was a fatal flaw: the evil spell of their breed was cast in darkness. If the light of day fell upon them, that spell was broken and the armour of their skin grew inwards. Their evil lives were crushed within, and they once again became lifeless stone.

Trolls were the evil antithesis of Ents in all things. Trolls were murderers and cannibals. Their diet was chiefly raw flesh. They often killed for pleasure – or for no reason at all. While Ents were made of living, growing wood, Trolls were made of hard, dead stone. Here was the root cause of an ancient war of attrition between wood and mountain. Treebeard once explained the difference: "Trolls are only counterfeits, made by the Enemy in the Great Darkness, in mockery of Ents, as Orcs were of Elves".

In the epic poem *Beowulf*, many troll-like creatures were tortured races thought to be the descendants of the cursed biblical murderer, Cain. Elsewhere in Anglo-Saxon literature, we have a jumble of words for a confusion of creatures that Tolkien shaped and standardized: "Eoten", meaning "giant" or "Ent" in Old English; "Jotunn", meaning "giant" in Old Norse; and "Troll", meaning "giant" or "monster" in Norse. For Trolls, Tolkien gives us a multitude of categories: Stone-Trolls, Cave-Trolls, Hill-Trolls, Mountain-Trolls, Forest-Trolls, and Snow-Trolls.

The stupidity of Trolls was so great that many could not be taught speech at all, while others learned the barest rudiments of the Black Speech. They hoarded treasure, but in the same way as crows might hoard bright jewels or shiny coins. They often worked in concert with Orcs and Uruks. Sadly, murderous stupidity combined with brutal strength in a narrow mountain pass or on a dark trail in a deep wood proved a remarkably effective combination to unwary travellers.

Myths and fairy tales

Trolls are found throughout the Scandinavian fairy-tale tradition. Scandinavian trolls were taller than the mountains and had fir trees growing out of their heads. They were the evil spirits of the mountains and forests. Known as ogres, windigos, gluttons, or titans, these trolls were present in every region of the world. They left their footprints all over the landscape, played with boulders as discuses, and changed

Right The Three Trolls episode in *The Hobbit* is reminiscent of *The Brave Little Tailor* by the Brothers Grimm. Sent to kill two terrible giants, the tailor finds them sleeping and throws stones at them, thus causing them to turn on each other and kill their supposed attacker.

Below An Olog-hai, a "super-Troll" similarly ferocious to the standard Troll, but capable of going out into daylight without being turned into stone.

the course of rivers. All are closely connected with the powers of the Earth usually living beneath mountains or in forest caves. Malevolent and often comic, these trolls were of massive size and strength, but were so stupid that they usually suffered humiliation and defeat at the hands of the puniest, but slightly cleverer, human opponents – some of whom were children and, in one particularly memorable case, a family of billy goats.

In fairy tales, trolls often possessed stolen treasure: a hoard of gold and gems, or perhaps a singing harp or an enchanted sword. Other trolls demanded payment from travellers for passing through their forests, mountains, and bridges. Payment might be in money or children, or an impossible riddle or deed. Trolls in such tales were jokingly collectors and "Keepers of Troll Toll Bridges". In all cases, an unscrupulous clever-boots hero was required to trick, swindle, or steal from a rather sad troll. If it were not for little faults such as murder and cannibalism, one might almost feel sorry for this mentally challenged species.

Right Trolls appear in a variety of literary sources, from Anglo-Saxon legend, to the children's tale of *The Billy Goats Gruff*. Tolkien's trolls most closely resemble the trolls of Jotunheim in Norse legend, where the Jotun giantesses rode on the backs of wolves, using serpents as reins.

Similarly, in Norse myths, troll-like giants were unruly monsters bent on destruction. They lived in Jotunheim – Land of Giants – and wanted to seize sovereignty of the world from the gods. In ancient Greece, they were the sons of the Earth and fought against Zeus for control of the world.

The episode in *The Hobbit* where Bilbo Baggins and his companions encounter three Trolls and only narrowly escape through outwitting them was clearly based on the Brother Grimms' tale *The Brave Little Tailor*. Similar trickster tales also appear in Icelandic mythology where we encounter Loki, the trickster god, or god of mischief, one of the Jotunn giants. Baldur, son of Odin has a dream that makes him fear for his life. Upon telling the gods about his dream, Frigg, his mother, decides to ask all things living and dead not to harm Baldur. But she forgets to ask the mistletoe, thinking it too young and harmless. Loki finds out about this and tricks Baldur's twin, Bod, into firing an arrow made of mistletoe at his brother, thus killing him. Likewise, Trolls are also tricked into killing their companions, either directly or indirectly, in both *The Brave Little Tailor* and *The Hobbit*.

Dragon Broods and Hoards

Beowulf and Smaug the Golden

"The dragon had the trade-mark 'of Faerie' written plain upon him," declared JRR Tolkien in his celebrated lectures on the art and tradition of fairy tales. Tolkien believed that the dragon and his golden hoard lay deep in the heart of "Faerie". Certainly these magnificent monsters enriched the imagination and fired the spirit that created Middle-earth and its inhabitants. "I desired dragons with a profound desire" he declared.

When writing his fairy-tale adventure *The Hobbit*, Tolkien decided that a dragon was not only desirable, but essential to his world. Not just any dragon would do, however; for he wanted to hunt the monster into his den. It was not by any coincidence that the greatest source of dragon lore was near at hand in the form of the Old English epic poem *Beowulf*.

On first inspection, there are no obvious similarities between *The Hobbit* and *Beowulf*. There are strong parallels, however, in the plot structure of the dragonslaying episode in *Beowulf* and the dragonslaying episode that is found in *The Hobbit*. *Beowulf*'s dragon awakes when a thief enters the monster's den. The thief steals a jewelled cup from the treasure hoard as he flees for his life. This is duplicated by Bilbo Baggins's burglary in the Golden Dragon's treasury when the Hobbit also steals a jewelled cup from the treasure hoard. Both thieves avoid capture and escape the anger of the dragons themselves. In both tales, it is the nearby settlements that suffer the dragon's wrath.

It is up to their respective champions, Beowulf, and Bard the Bowman in *The Hobbit*, to slay the beast. Both heroes succeed in slaying their dragons, but at a cost. Bard survives to become King of Dale, while the older Beowulf does not long survive the conflict. Just as Sigmund the Volsung of the great Norse myth was to see his sword blade shatter in his last battle, so, too, Beowulf's fate was sealed when his sword "Nailing" broke in his struggle with the monster. Although victorious, Beowulf nevertheless dies of his wounds. Beowulf's death is mirrored in the *The Hobbit*, not by Bard, but by that other warrior king of the tale, the Dwarf Thorin Oakenshield, who is also victorious at the Battle of the Five Armies, but dies of his wounds.

The Hobbit is the *Beowulf* dragon story told from the thief's point of view. There is, however, one big problem with *Beowulf*'s dragon. He is more the admittedly terrifying embodiment of an evil curse than an individual villain who happens to be a dragon. All characters in a really good fairy-tale adventure must have something of a close-up, intimate feeling. This is true of all of an adventure's characters, even – or especially – the bad ones. The trouble with the *Beowulf* dragon is that the closer you come, the more it recedes. You cannot gain a hold on him: the monster did not even have a name.

For Tolkien, this was a cardinal sin. Within the spheres of Middle-earth names are primary factors in all life forms and the creation of all things. Tolkien began to feel like the maiden in *Rumplestiltskin* whose fate depended on discovering the creature's true name. With this end in mind, Tolkien came across an Old English phrase thought to be a riddle, or a spell, to ward off dragons. The phrase read: "wid smeogan wyrme", which in translation means "against the penetrating worm".

Tolkien liked the sound of the word: *smeogan*. He also liked the depth of ambiguity in its meaning: "penetrating". It sounded like something either amusing or serious, or both at once. Yet it was not a name. As a grammarian, Tolkien observed that smeogan was an adjective and therefore, strictly speaking, could not be considered a name. Still, Tolkien knew that he was on the right trail. With the scent of the unnamed beast unmistakeably in his nostrils, Tolkien let loose the hounds of philology and gave chase.

From the perceptive, but unfortunately adjectival, "smeogan", the scent led to the thoughtful "smeagan", meaning "to inquire into". From there, it was not difficult to bring to earth a poor relation, the pushy "smeogol" – "worming into" – as well as its verbal and sneaky "smugan" – "to creep through". Now in hot pursuit, Tolkien knew of another "smugan", an older and less active ancestor in a bordering language. As all three members of this Old English family proved to have a common ancestor, the chase was resumed in the ancient phantom forest of prehistoric German. There the secretive, cave-dwelling "Smugan" – which means "to squeeze through a hole" – was at last brought to bay. After a short interrogation, it was revealed that in ancient days he had indeed been the very dragon, but no longer. Those days were gone, unless the pursuers knew the secret word which would allow him to return to the past.

The secretive "Smugan" was no match for the wily Tolkien, who guessed his meaning in a moment. By converting the prehistoric German verb to its past tense, Smugan was "squeezed through a hole' back in time. And so, the riddle was solved: the name of the dragon had to be "Smaug"! Yé! utúvienyes!

SMAUG! Smaug the Golden! Now that was a name! Yes, this was better than a large but nameless lizard. Smaug the Magnificent carried the collective meaning of its composite parts in Old English: penetrating, inquiring, burrowing, worming into, and creeping through. These were all useful clues to a really slippery, intelligent, and nasty villain. Then, too, came an appropriate – if accidental – pun on smog, which insinuates its way through as a distinctive whiff of brimstone.

Right Ancalagon the Black was the first of the Winged Dragons on Middle-earth, and was bred by Morgoth in the Pits of Angband.

Dragon eye and serpent tale

In the writing of *The Hobbit*, JRR Tolkien discovered "a profound desire" for dragons was becoming focused on "a desire for a profound dragon". In the creation of the winged, fire-breathing dragon, Tolkien looked into all that philology could teach him about dragons and all that he considered the best of dragon lore.

Once again, Tolkien used the names of things as a journey of discovery. Tolkien chose to begin with the name of the beast. Dragon is taken directly from the Greek *drakon*, which simply means "serpent", but is derived from the Greek word *drakein*, meaning "look, glance, flash, gleam". Thus, the Greek *drakon* "to see fiercely" and the idea of a watcher or fierce guardian. Similarly, the Sanskrit *darc* implies a "creature that looks on you with a deadly glance". In Greek too, the words for dragon, or great serpent, convey the sense of a "Watcher with a Deadly Glance" that is also a guardian of a treasure or a sacred site. These words also suggest a creature with the capacity to see prophetic visions and to "see" in the sense of possessing ancient, arcane knowledge.

Dragons are also commonly known as worms. In Old English and Norse literature, and indeed most European mythology, dragon and worm are used interchangeably to describe the same monster. Consequently each transfers layers of meaning from the other. The word "worm", however, has a very different root meaning related to the physical characteristics of snakes and serpents. The English "worm", Old English "wyrm", Old Norse "ormr", Gothic "waurms", and Latin "vermis" all come from the root "wer", meaning "turn, twist". Therefore, the word or name "worm" carries the meaning of an elemental "twisting, turning creature".

Snakes and serpents are also twisting and turning creatures, and, in most modern languages of northern Europe, these words became entwined with the word "worm" and its variations: *Wurm* is the German for snake; *worm* is the Dutch for snake; and *orm* means snake in both Danish and Swedish. Snake and serpent, however, come from different root meanings, which add other dimensions to our composite monster. Snake is from the prehistoric German root *Snag*, meaning "crawl"; while serpent is from the Latin *serpere*, meaning "crawl, creep".

To all the sinister qualities gained by way of the naming of Smaug, we now add a multitude of aspects: a watcher and fierce guardian of treasury; a creature that looks on with a deadly glance; a twisting, turning creature; a creature of prophetic vision; a keeper of arcane knowledge; a creeping crawling creature; and a being whose eyes gleam, glance, and flash. Whatever one wishes to make of a composite creature with these qualities, it will be something both terrifying and mesmerizing. It is certain that from this hoard of words Smaug the Magnificent inherited his laser eyes, brilliant intellect, mesmerizing spells, and not a few of his other more terrifying qualities.

In the creation of Smaug the Golden, we see the perfect fairy-tale dragon: a villain of great charm, intelligence, and vanity. A flying, fire-breathing dragon whose terrible wrath and vengeance is somehow still admired as one might observe a truly spectacular fireworks display. The reason for this is the playful nature of such creatures in true fairy tales where, no matter how fearful, one knows that the flying terror will be overcome and that nearly every really good person is guaranteed a happy ending.

Fafnir and Glaurung, the father of dragons

The adventures of Smaug could not, however, be an event without precedence. Everything comes from somewhere, and dragons come from somewhere very ancient and very evil. This was a brutal and primitive world akin to that revealed in the earliest Old German epics which do not knowingly record one happy ending in a millennium of brilliant – if thematically foredoomed – literary achievement.

Nonetheless, within this shadowy world of guaranteed tragic ending, Tolkien began to cast about for a dragon appropriate to the setting. Smaug was far too charming and amusing. (And in any case Smaug was chronologically a later creation.) Tolkien required something that was brutal, murderous, and filled with low cunning. He wanted something that wallowed in the pleasures of torture of mind, body, and soul. Tolkien knew exactly what he wanted and where to find it: the embodiment of something akin to the most evil of all monsters created by the collective imaginations of the German and Norse races.

Few would disagree with Tolkien in his *On Fairy Stories* when it came to the dragon of dragons: "best of all [was] the nameless North of Sigurd of the Volsungs, and the prince of all dragons". This "prince of all dragons" was the spectacularly patricidal, fratricidal, genocidal – and deeply unpleasant – Fafnir the Fire-Drake, the

Below Although unable to fly as later dragons would be able to do, Glaurung, the very first dragon in Middle-earth, possessed huge destructive power with his breath of fire.

usurper of the cursed golden treasure of the (mysterious and extinct) Nibelungs. However evil, Tolkien believed that "the world that contained even the imagination of Fafnir was richer and more beautiful, at whatever cost of peril".

In the hero, Túrin Turambar, we have the first of Middle-earth's Dragonslayers, and a story redolent of the tales of other nations. In part, Túrin resembles the cursed hero Kullervo from the Finnish epic the *Kalevala*. A tortured soul, unloved from birth, Kullervo was blessed with powerful sorcery, which he used to punish his enemies. Like Túrin, Kullervo unwittingly slept with his long-lost sister and, unable to cope with the guilt, also fell on his sword. There are also repeated motifs from the tragedy of Oedipus: he too, defeated a great monster (the Sphinx) and unknowingly married his mother, Jocasta.

Most of all, Túrin shares many similarities with the Norse hero Sigurd the Dragonslayer in *The Volsunga Saga*. The son of King Sigmund and Queen Hjordis, Sigurd had a mentor in the master smith Regin, just as Túrin had in the warrior Beleg Strongbow. It is Regin who challenges Sigurd to slay Fafnir, the mighty dragon, and, just as Túrin ambushed Glaurung (the father of Middle-earth's dragons) in the Brethil Forest, so Sigurd finds Fafnir in the evil forest of Mirkwood (a name also used by Tolkien). Digging a trench in the dragon's path, Sigurd waited for Fafnir to pass above him before thrusting his sword up into the dragon's soft belly. And just as Túrin's great triumph was soured by the truth about his sister-lover, Nienor, so Sigurd's slaying of Fafnir is tempered by the treachery of Regin, who is planning to kill him and claim the dragon's gold for himself. After tasting Fafnir's heartblood, Sigurd can suddenly understand the birds discussing Regin's scheme. Sigurd kills Regin and his legend as dragonslayer is complete.

Edain – Men of the First Age

Hildórien – awakening of Men

The First Age of the Sun was a heroic age of Middle-earth, a time that draws comparison with the great stories of Greek and Viking myth. There are echoes of the classical heroes of Greece, characters such as Hercules, who were set impossible tasks and labours, yet somehow managed to achieve them through a combination of physical strength and mental determination. There are similarities, too, with the heroes of the Norse legends, particularly their characteristics of hardiness and fighting spirit, facing death with vigour and courage. Nowhere is this more apparent than when it comes to *The Volsunga Saga* – described by William Morris as "the great story of the North, which should be to all our race what the tale of Troy was to the Greeks". Tolkien used its central hero, Sigurd the Dragonslayer, as the basis for his Elf-friend warrior, Túrin Turambar.

Just as the coming of the Ages of the Sun was a sign for the coming of Men, however, it was also to see the last days of Sindar, the greatest Elf Kingdom on Middle-earth. The High King Thingol and his Queen, Melian the Maia, had a daughter who was considered the most beautiful maiden of any race ever born and the fairest singer within the Spheres of the World. For this she was named Lúthien Tinúviel, meaning "maiden of twilight", around whom the nightingales gathered. Like Arwen Evenstar later in *The Lord of the Rings*, Lúthien is the very embodiment of a "lady in white", a common feature of Celtic legend. In the Welsh legend of the wooing of Olwyn, Olwyn too is considered the most beautiful woman of her age. Her eyes, like Lúthien's, shine with light; her skin is also as white as snow. Olwyn's name means "she of the white track" because four white trefoils sprang up on the forest floor for every step she took: the Niphredil is a white star-shaped flower that first bloomed on Middle-earth in celebration of Lúthien's birth and blossomed eternally on her burial mound. The winning of Olwyn's hand required the near-impossible gathering of the "Treasure of Britain": in order to be allowed to wed Lúthien, the Silmaril had to be captured by her suitor.

As Tolkien saw it, "there is a strand of 'blood' and inheritance, derived from the Elves, and that the art and poetry of Men is largely dependent on it, or modified by it". The wisdom and history of the immortal Elves are the Myth Age inheritance of Men, an inheritance which is the ennobling spirit of human civilizations. Crucial to establishing this link between Elves and Men was the betrothal of the beautiful maiden Lúthien to the mortal hero Beren, a betrothal that forced them into the Quest of the Silmaril.

Beleriand – heroic age of Elf-friends

This inheritance, passed on through "a strain of blood" gained through intermarriage of Men and Elves in the First Age, was manifest in the Myth Age of the Primary World with the intermarriage of gods and heroes, as described in the legends of Gilgamish the Sumerian, Hercules of Greece, Kullervo the Finn, Sigurd the Volsung, and Cúchulainn of Ireland.

Kullervo is the most significant of these, as in its origin, *The Silmarillion* was to be based on the Finnish national epic, the *Kalevala*. And Tolkien indeed creates a narrative redolent of the northern legends. In the ill-fated Edain hero Túrin Turambar (ironically named "Master of Doom" by the Grey Elves), there is a strong resemblance to the foredoomed and cursed Finnish hero Kullervo. Both heroes are Dragonslayers and caught up by some ill fate that leads them to murder and incest. As Tolkien mentioned, Túrin and Kullervo shared the big triple "incest-murder-dragon" theme with Sigurd the Dragonslayer. Tolkien also acknowledged the Greek king Oedipus as an influence, whose monster was the equally deadly Sphinx of Thebes.

The influence of Finnish language and literature on *The Silmarillion* has been quite considerable, and was repeated by Tolkien on a number of occasions throughout his works. He wrote that the *Kalavala* was the original germ of *The Silmarillion* and that the High Elvish tongue of Quenya is a kind of Elvish Latin, based on the linguistically similar Finnish. Names like Ilúvatar and Ulmo are intended to be suggestive of the Finnish names Ilmarinen and Ilmo from the *Kalevala*; the Valar of Middle-earth are the powers who have been "bounded in the world", and "vala" in Finnish means "bond".

It is therefore almost inevitable that the mysterious prize of both epics seems equally obscure. In the *Kalevla* the great prize that has brought tragedy to many is called the "Sampo". It is something of a riddle: it is the work of the master-smith Ilmarinen, handed over as payment for a bride. When it was stolen back, it was broken in the pursuit, and survived only in fragments. No one knows what it is – or rather, what it was, for its loss is irrevocable and complete. This is obviously similar to the Silmarils, which were also forged by a master-smith, Fëanor the Noldor. Meanwhile, philologists suggest the Sampo is variously something bright, something made in a forge, a kind of mill, a thing that brings luck, or something to do with sea salt.

Some have suggested it is something like the Golden Fleece, or even the Holy Grail, believed to be the Chalice used by Christ at the Last Supper. The Grail, in the many stories surrounding it, has become an elusve and enigmatic symbol; it doesn't belong in this world as it is far too pure for mortal beings. Only Galahad was pure enough to lift it, but then both he and the Grail ascended straight to heaven. Good in itself, the Grail ruined Camelot and many good knights died pursuing it. Tolkien surmised the Sampo was at once both an object and an allegory – real and yet abstract. He saw it also as the quintessence of the creative powers, capable of provoking both good and evil. His Silmarils were intended as objects of similarly intense but obscure symbolism, focal points of the inexorable pattern of fate.

Insofar as the Grail, the Sampo and the Silmarils had a purpose, it seems to have been to remind all created beings that the mystery of ultimate destiny and purpose was something they could not penetrate. And yet they all generated an ardent yearning to find them and hold them. And here there is a paradox, since although all three shine with divine light, yet they have often provoked a descent in the opposite direction by those who have pursued them.

The power of love – Orpheus and Lúthien

Where thousands had perished before them, Beren and Lúthien passed through the gates of Angband and down to the great hall and iron throne of Morgoth. Lúthien's enchanted song made Carcharoth the wolf-guardian fall asleep before the gates of Morgoth's dark subterranean kingdom. Once within, Lúthien again sang such beautiful songs that she and Beren won the Silmaril jewel from Morgoth, the lord of the underworld. Lúthien succeeded in fleeing from the underworld, but at the last moment, at the mouth of the tunnel, she lost her lover Beren.

The "Quest of the Silmaril" and related tales of Beren and Lúthien are among the very first tales of Middle-earth, which Tolkien began just before the First World War. Beren and Lúthien's descent into Angband is Tolkien's Myth-Time prototype for what is, quite literally, the oldest story in the world: that of the courageous descent into the kingdom of the dead, the power of enchanting music to persuade a captive to be released, and the discovery that true eternity lies in the purity and power of love. It was Tolkien's most personally cherished legend, as a result of his own forced separation and the near loss of his true love, Edith Bratt. On his and his wife Edith's grave stone it states simply: "John Ronald Ruel Tolkien (1892–1973) Beren"; "Edith Bratt Tolkien (1889–1971) Lúthien".

The oldest version of this story was discovered in the 5000-year-old Mesopotamian tale of the goddess Ianna surviving the "Descent and Harrowing of Hell". It is a tale repeated with some variations in the myth of the Babylonian Goddess Astarte. Astarte is the morning and evening star – the planet Venus – who makes the descent to rescue her lover Thammuz. The myth of the Assyrian goddess Ishtar – again the planet Venus – recounts a terrifying ordeal. She is layer by layer stripped and skinned alive as she descends through the seven gates of the seven walls of hell – all

Right The story of Beren and Lúthien, seen here before the throne of Morgoth (Beren in the form of a wolf), bears a close resemblance to the Greek myth of Orpheus and Eurydice.

that remains of her is blood and bone. Yet she endures to rescue her lover, Tammuz the golden-haired corn god. In the Egyptian tale, Isis, the Queen of goddesses, descends into the Underworld to resurrect and rescue the king of the gods, her husband Osiris. Best known to westerners is the Greek myth of the goddess Demeter who descends into Hades to rescue the goddess of Spring, her daughter Persephone.

It is not until the myth of Orpheus and Eurydice that the theme of the power of music and the descent to the underworld are joined as one – as they are in the tale of Beren and Lúthien. The male and females roles are the reverse of the Greek myth, but the Orpheus version is the reverse of virtually all the other versions. Orpheus played his harp and sang to make Cerberus the hound guardian fall asleep before the gates of Hades' dark subterranean kingdom. Once within, Orpheus again sang such beautiful songs that he won the life of Eurydice from Hades, the lord of the underworld. Orpheus succeeded in fleeing the underworld, but at the last

Below The character of Sigurd from the Norse Ring Legend, *The Volsunga Saga*, who slays the dragon Fafnir by digging a trench and thrusting his sword up into the dragon's belly, undoubtedly inspired Tolkien's portrayal of the dragonslayer Túrin Turambar.

moment, at the mouth of the tunnel, he lost his lover Eurydice, when, against Hades' instructions, he looked back to check that she was still following.

Orpheus was the son of the King of Thrace, some time around the beginning of the sixth century BC. He was an accomplished lyre player and enchanting singer. He became famous as a poet and a musician, and the effects of his music were both enchanting and extraordinary. He bewitched gods, men, wild animals and birds, and even inanimate objects such as stones and mountains. Trees leaned over as he passed to hear his mesmerising music. In his journey with Jason and the other Argonauts, he sang to the elements when faced with terrible storms, and brought on calm through the sweet harmony of song. Using his art, he overcame the Sirens' bewitching songs by which they entrapped mortal men, then destroyed their spells. He returned his companions to the straight path – just as Eärendil the Mariner by the power of the light of the Silmaril sailed the "Straight Road" in his own quest.

In the cult of Orpheus, we are told that the singer brought back from his long stay in the Underworld a wealth of knowledge about overcoming death, avoiding eternal damnation, and reaching the land of the blessed. These revelations were circulated in a great deal of literature, hymns, epics, and poems, and a great intellectual movement came into existence. Tolkien's protagonists gain vision, wisdom and depth of character from the same experience.

The silmaril – Venus and the star of Eärendil

So, upon Middle-earth, the Silmaril was the symbol of the salvation of the Elves and Men. It eventually ended up upon the brow of Eärendil as he sailed his ship through the skies. This is the light that is called the morning star and is also the evening star. It is the living light that is the planet named Venus the Goddess of Love. The "flame of the west", it is a sign of hope and love to all who look upon it.

The origins of the character of Eärendil, as we saw earlier, can be traced back to Tolkien's undergraduate days, when he came across a group of Anglo-Saxon poems known as the "Crist of Cynewulf". For some, the story of Eärendil resonates with a minor character from Norse mythology, the warrior Aurvandil the Brave. Husband of the seeress Groa, Aurvandil was carried across the poisonous waters of the Elivager by the mighty warrior Thor. But when one of Aurvandil's toes freezes, Thor snaps it off and throws it into the heavens to create a new star. This star, known as Aurvandil's Toe, is most likely the morning star – the same star central to the tale of Eärendil.

There are also echoes in Greek myth of the twin brothers Castor and Pollux. Like Eärendil's children, Elros and Elrond, Castor and Pollux have one mortal parent (Leda) and one immortal (Zeus). When Castor is killed in battle, his immortal

Above In Greek legend, Orpheus lulls the three-headed dog, Cerberus, to sleep in order to enter Hades the Underworld. Similarly, Lúthien gains a second life for herself and Beren by singing in the House of the Dead in the Undying Lands.

brother Pollux is so distraught at not seeing him again that Zeus takes pity and transforms the twins into the constellation Gemini. In Tolkien's tale, however, it is the father and not the sons who ends up a star. There is also perhaps a link between Elwing and characters from Greek mythology. Just as Elwing, who loves Eärendil, is turned into a white seabird by Ulmo, the Valarian Ocean Lord, so Zeus, who loves the mortal Leda, comes to her disguised as a swan. In Tolkien's great tapestry there are also hints of Celtic legend. The Elven Elwing's transformation into a white seabird and her carriage of the Silmaril in her beak is possibly another reference to the pre-human Irish race of immortals known as the Tuatha Dé Danann with whom Tolkien's Elves are associated, as we have already seen. The remnants of this once mighty race were the Aes Sidhe, or Sidhe (pronounced "Shee") who had a strong affinity with starlight. When the children of Lír, part ocean god, part earthly king, are spitefully transformed by Aoife, their wicked stepmother, it is the shape of swans that they assume.

Lúthien and Arwen

The resemblances between the stories of these two beautiful heroines, Elven or Half-elven, have been noted already, and of course, are no coincidence. Both renounce immortality in order to unite themselves to a mortal man of heroic character. Some critics have regretted the passive part played by Arwen in the Ring story, compared to the active and crucial role of Lúthien in *The Silmarillion*. Indeed, in one of the few departures from Tolkien's story-line made by the film version of *The Fellowship of the Ring*, Peter Jackson gives Arwen a dramatic part in facing down the Black Riders. But, as the story of Éowyn shows, Tolkien had no objection to placing a woman right in the heart of battle. If Arwen remains in Rivendell, it must be seen as part of the author's whole plan. In the context of Tolkien's entire time scheme, Lúthien is an archaic figure, from the earliest age, with a mythic quality that adds poignancy to her assumption of humanity. Arwen lives close to the other end of the time-scale. She is in a sense more "real" to us than her illustrious but remote ancestress. And her part is a more modern one, that we can understand: it is that of the woman who must stay at home while her lover goes to risk his life – and her happiness – in a war which he seems very unlikely to survive. It has a different and more immediate poignancy, the anguish of watching and waiting. That is not the whole significance of Arwen, of course. In a sense she too is a concealed treasure, glowing, as her 'Evenstar' name suggests, in a hidden place. But this treasure, too, could fall into the wrong hands, if the actions of Men or Elves go awry, or if fate so determines.

Númenóreans –
Men of the Second Age

The downfall of Atlantis

This age, the Second Age, began with a dream, a "terrible recurrent dream", which Tolkien interpreted as an inherited racial memory. In describing the effect of this dream on Tolkien, one might use the same words that he used in reaction to Eärendil's star: "something stirred in me, half wakened from sleep". It was the dark terror of a nightmare that "half wakened" him to a vivid belief in the reality of an ancient disaster.

In the histories of the mighty Sea Kings of the island nation of Númenor which so dominated the Second Age, we find Tolkien motivated by a personal vision. It should come as no surprise to us that Tolkien believed that some myths were essentially inherited racial memories of ancient historic events. Tolkien truly enters the realm of the mystic, however, with his belief that he had inherited an ancient memory through his dreams.

From early childhood, Tolkien experienced one recurring nightmare: "… of the Great Wave, towering up, and coming in ineluctably over the trees and green fields." What was most frightening, even in his "half wakened" state was the feeling that it was more a vivid memory than a bad dream. Tolkien felt that he had somehow personally experienced the event. It was not until he came to read the legend of the fall of Atlantis that Tolkien recognized this as the disaster behind his dark dream of the "Great Wave". However, Tolkien never wished to discuss this "terrible recurring dream", especially not with his children. As a result, Tolkien did not learn until years later that, remarkably, his son Michael had experienced in early childhood the same recurring dream of the "Great Wave".

Tolkien's ideas of racial memory extended to the recognition of ancestral languages. As he once explained to WH Auden: "I am a West-midlander by blood (and took to early west-midland Middle English as a known tongue as soon as I set eyes on it),…." For Auden, the idea of a language unspoken for seven centuries being recognized as a "known tongue" had a charm and an aesthetic truth, delightful to poets and spiritualists. It is the sort of illogical nonsense, however, that drives most disciplined academics – philologists aside – to distraction; it is considered to be indicative of heresy or lunacy, or both.

Such charges do not appear to have affected Tolkien at all. He remained immune to any suggested adjustment to his beliefs. He appears to have believed in the actual physical existence of the island kingdom of Atlantis and the legend of its spectacular disappearance.

Left The legend of a lost island civilization is one of the most enduring in human history. Atlantis is believed to have been constructed in concentric circles, connected by bridges over canals, up to a great temple in the centre. The whole island was dominated by a great volcano, and was finally destroyed by a huge tidal wave.

The earliest recorded legend of Atlantis comes from Plato's *Timaeus* in which an Egyptian priest talks to the Athenian statesman Solon. The priest tells Solon that the mightiest civilization the world had ever known existed 9000 years before his time on the island-kingdom of Atlantis. Atlantis was the size of Spain, and was located in the western sea beyond the Pillars of Hercules. Atlantis' power extended to all nations of the world, but the Tyrant of Atlantis brings his nation into conflict with the laws of the Immortals. Socrates' description of the conflict is expressed in terms of a musical allegory. Like Melkor in the "Music of the Ainur", the Tyrant brings such discord to the harmony of the world that Socrates calls it the "diabolus in musica": the "devil in the music". Like the walls of Jericho, the foundation stones of the Isle of Atlantis begin to crack. Zeus is called to pass judgment. We are never told the judgment, but Atlantis has vanished from the face of our Earth. Tolkien's narrative bears testimony to the validity of the widespread myth of a single civilization that inspired all Mankind though its achievements in arts and sciences.

Empire of the Sea Kings

The Second Age was the era of the mighty Sea Kings of Númenor, the "Land of the Star". In High Elvish, the name of their kingdom was Atalantë or, as the ancient Greeks knew it, Atlantis. In his histories, Tolkien presents the "true" history of the fate of Atlantis. The first king of the Númenóreans was Elros. Elros and Elrond were the twin sons of Eärendil the Mariner and the Elven Princess Elwing. As the

Below While Númenor burns and crumbles into the sea, a few inhabitants manage to escape in nine ships and sail to Middle-earth where, as the Dúnedain, they will found the kingdoms of Gondor and Arnor.

offspring of a mortal and an immortal, they became known as the Peredhil ("half-elven twins"). They have their counterpart in Greek mythology in Castor and Pollux, who were known as the "heavenly twins" – the Dioscuri – or, more commonly, when they were placed among the stars, the Gemini. Like the Dioscuri, because of their mixed blood, the Peredhil were given the choice of mortal or immortal lives.

Just as Tolkien used certain biblical themes that connected the Elves with the Hebrew tribes of Moses, so the mortal Númenóreans had associations with the biblical Egyptians. (Like Moses's people, the Elves are a "chosen people" who endured terrible hardships on their journey to the "promised land"). In a letter in the late 1950s, Tolkien wrote: "The Númenóreans of Gondor were proud, peculiar, and archaic, and I think are best pictured in (say) Egyptian terms." There is a similarity, too, between the ultimate fate of Númenor and what happens to the Pharaoh of Egypt's army in their pursuit of the Hebrews of Moses.

Númenor was the "land of the gift" and "the land of the star", roughly shaped like a pentagram – a five-pointed star. This star shape is sometimes known as the "Star of Man" because its five points relate to a body outstretched: the head at the top, the arms and hands at the side, and the legs and feet at the bottom.

Corrupted by Sauron, the Númenóreans became so proud that they wanted immortality. This would have brought such discord to the Spheres that Ilúvatar caused the land to burst asunder and Númenor collapsed into a watery abyss. This was the second fall of man, as it was to the nations of the world during the time of Noah and the Great Flood.

Those who managed to escape were the Dúnedain ("Men of the West") who established the north and south kingdoms of Arnor and Gondor. The powerful Black Númenóreans also survived and made a great haven in Umbar on the southern coast of Middle-earth. They became a mighty sea power and made war upon the Dúnedain, bringing hoardes of barbarians with them. As we shall explore in greater detail later, the parallels with European history are marked: the civilized northern European lands of the Carolingian and Holy Roman Empires being under attack from the Moors, Saracens and Turks from the south and east.

Númenor's rise is a paradigm of the growth of empires. But its fall is of the kind more often found recorded of mighty individuals who grow too proud, or bold. This, in ancient Greek terms, was hubris, contempt for the gods, traditionally punished with extreme severity. The tradition of a universal deluge is an ancient one and may have its origins in the raising of the sea levels which followed the end of the last ice age, about 10,000 years ago; or it may relate to the effects of a colossal Santorini-like volcanic explosion. Its oldest known version is found in the Assyrian tablets which record the story of Gilgamesh, king of Erech.

Dream wave enters history

In the Second Age, Tolkien as a spinner of tales is caught up in the conscious attempt to reinvent the "true history" behind the destruction of Atlantis, a legend that has so much in common with so many of the world's mythologies. Tolkien appears to be almost too clever in the way he has woven this tale. However much Tolkien works this story into a "legend on the brink of fairy tale and history", at the same time he obviously believed in Atlantis as a genuine historic event. More than that, it is a clear case of Tolkien's personal revelations invading and motivating his tales in order to "prove" the authenticity of the story of Númenor as an analogy for an historic Atlantis.

As Tolkien once wrote: "History often resembles 'Myth', because they are both ultimately made of the same stuff." Remarkably, Tolkien managed to live just long enough to have the historicity of the sudden cataclysmic destruction of a lost Atlantis-like civilization proved accurate, as well as his description of the "Great Wave" which followed in its wake. In the mid-1960s, excavations of the Aegean revealed an island kingdom which was destroyed in the second millennium BC by a volcanic eruption and a great wave. This tidal wave devastated the entire Mediterranean from Greece to Morocco and Spain. Thera – now known as Santorini – had been the centre of the Minoan Empire, yet it was destroyed in a single cataclysmic event in a single day. All its cities, its fleets, and its entire population vanished beneath the sea. The Age of the Sea Kings came to an end as the largest tidal wave ever witnessed by humankind struck the island's shores.

So it seems that this terror of the Great Wave had flooded out of Tolkien's personal nightmare into a legend, then into Middle-earth, before bursting back in upon human history. Or perhaps, as Tolkien suggested, the sequence ran in the opposite order, beginning in Middle-earth. Whatever the case, Tolkien's belief in this recurring dream did result in the composition of the annals of the Sea Kings of Númenor and their kingdom, which in later (or earlier, since Tolkien wants us to believe that his mythology of Middle-earth precedes that of the ancient Greeks) days was known by the ancient Greeks as Atlantis. However, that was not the nightmare's end. Just as Tolkien's own son, Michael, had inherited the dream, so we discover in *The Lord of the Rings* that, millennia later, a descendant of the Sea Kings has inherited a horrific vision of the downfall of Númenor. In the War of the Ring, Faramir the Stewart of Gondor watches the destruction of Sauron. Faramir confesses that it reminds him of a recurring dream "of the great dark wave climbing over green lands… coming on, darkness inescapable".

Dúnedain — Men of the Third Age

The seven circles of the city

"Seven stars and seven stones and one white tree." These were the words of a song that were a puzzle to the Hobbits, Merry and Pippin; however, the riddle was in part solved when, in Gondor, these Hobbits entered the City of the White Tower. The structure of the city of Gondor in seven circles, the livery of the Guards of the Citadel which featured seven stars, the presence of the White Tree of the Elves and one of the seven Palantíri in the city are all symbols of the Dúnedain's ancient Elven heritage of wisdom and culture.

The City was shaped rather like a massive stone musical pitch-pipe or a three-dimensional musical octave marked out by its great walls as seven stone circles: a

Right The beautiful city of Minas Tirith, built by the Dúnedian in concentric circles that perhaps harkened back to the structure of their ancestral kingdom of Númenor. Tolkien gave the city a location within the geography of Middle-earth that reveals his perception of it as the "Florence" of Middle-earth.

massive earthly cross-section of the seven celestial spheres. Indeed, one answer to the phrase of the song that so puzzled the Hobbits could lie in the Music of the Spheres, which Tolkien drew upo as we have already seen. The seven stars could be interpreted as the seven crystal spheres that are the source of the Great Music wherein all that is and will be are to be found. As for the seven stones, these could be seen as seven crystal balls wherein a small part of the wisdom of the Great Music may be revealed.

Another reason for the seven circles of Minas Tirith could come from the ancestry of the city's inhabitants. Those who survived the end of Númenor brought with them the knowledge and wisdom of that doomed kingdom. In the same way that Atlantis, with which Númenor shares so many similarities, was built on seven concentric circles of islands, so perhaps the structure of Minas Tirith was an echo of this lost land of Númenor.

The notion of Minas Tirith as the guardian of ancient wisdom bears testament to Tolkien's intention of making the city a Middle-earth equivalent of the Renaissance city-state of Florence. Certainly in Minas Tirith, there are echoes of the great Italian city, home of the Medici and centre of the Renaissance. Florence's role in the humanism of the sixteenth century was crucial, rescuing and rehabilitating the texts of the ancient world. Here, in a city of domes and palaces, works of art and manuscripts of the ancient world were preserved and cherished. Many of its relics came with the refugees from a recent disaster, the final conquest of Constantinople by the Seljuk Turks in 1453, and with it the eclipse of its long-retained Greek culture.

But Osgiliath is a ruin, and Minas Anor has become Minas Tirith, the Tower of Guard. Gondor is is only a fragment of what it once had been. It is easy, but wrong, to read a description of Great Britain, and its former empire, into this. At the time Tolkien was writing *The Lord of the Rings*, the sense of a British Empire was still strong. He could more probably have had the fate of the Austrian Empire in mind: from 1918, Vienna, for centuries a proud imperial metropolis, was reduced to being the capital of a single small country. Its emperor was dethroned. In Gondor too, there is no king, only the Steward. Tolkien had ancestral reasons for being interested in Austria, as we shall see later. However, history is full of examples of fallen empires and broken dynasties. Rome is an eloquent example. The broken columns and shattered arches of ancient Rome have a powerful echo in the destroyed architecture and noble ruins of Gondor, as well as in the sternness and clear, harsh code of life of those who still maintain the old tradition.

Survivors of the cataclysm

Just as the story of Atlantis has echoes in many mythologies from around the world, so too does the creation of a new kingdom from the survivors of such a cataclysm.

The Mayas of Central America, for example, claim to be descendants of those who escaped the submerging of Aztlan. Celtic tales tell of ancestors originating from the sunken land of Cantref Gwaelod. And in the Bible, of course, there is the story of Noah and the Great Flood. The people of the divided kingdoms of Arnor and Gondor are the descendants of the Númenóreans who fled the destruction of their island kingdom.

"Sundering" is a word that recurs in Tolkien's works, and always with a tragic cast to it. The notion of separation was clearly something that affected him profoundly. In his stories there are many examples of the distress, turmoil and disasters that arise from separation. One of the main forces underlying his thought can be detected here. Continuance of separation leads to tragic events, or, as with the eventual retreat of the Elves, to a kind of mutedly tragic tone. Unification, if it can be achieved, leads to positive results, joy and contentment. At the beginning of the Ring events, the race of Men is a sundered one, with no contacts between the people of Gondor and their dispersed northern kindred. By the end, they are united as one people again, with the promise of peace, harmony, and the rule of law.

United under one king

Kingship in the world of Middle-earth is something very important. To all its peoples, monarchy is the natural political condition. Kings were not like ordinary men. This is an old tradition in English thought; England remains a staunchly monarchic country in a world of presidencies, and JRR Tolkien was a thorough royalist in his sympathies. Shakespeare had written in Hamlet about how "divinity doth hedge a king". In Tolkien it is rather the inherent qualities in the man himself which exalt him. Even when a king goes utterly to the bad, as with the Witch-king of Angmar, he retains his kingly quality and powers of leadership. Although a king may seem old and weak, like Théoden, his royal gift remains; he can shake these things off and resume strength and command. (Incidentally, readers of George Macdonald's *The Princess and Curdie* will see a certain debt to the story there of the old king, long kept in a sort of stupor by his wicked servants). And a king has a certain superhuman quality: he has healing powers, the doctor of his people as well as their leader. In England too, well into the eighteenth century, the touch of the reigning monarch was believed to heal the tuberculosis-related condition of scrofula. All these qualities are seen at their height in the figure of Aragorn. But in him there is also a memory of something far earlier and more fundamental in kingship.

Ancient human societies had a king for a year only. Chosen or self-presented in the spring, he was crowned, feted and given everything he could be provided with. And then, late in the autumn, they killed him, so that his blood would fertilise the

Left The Gates of Gondor, the Argonath, were two monolithic carvings of the first kings of Gondor. They marked the northern boundary of the kingdom above the great Rauros Falls on the Anduin River.

Far left Isildur holds the shattered sword Narsil, with which he cut the One Ring from the hand of Sauron. The broken or reforged sword, and the sword with magical powers are motifs common in many medieval European legends.

soil. "The king is dead, long live the king" is a very old saying. It was to bring back such "corn-kings" that the ancient goddesses made their descents into the underworld. In the story of Aragorn, the "return of the king" has an obvious meaning, but also a mythic one. Before he comes to Minas Tirith to be acknowledged as king of Gondor, he too passes through a form of underworld, in his journey through the Paths of the Dead (and it is to them that he first unfurls the standard Arwen has made for him, though in the darkness it cannot be seen by his companions). His ordeal was necessary to make him fit and eligible to perform the role of a true king in making his country great and prosperous again, as he indeed proceeds to do.

Hobbits of the Shire

Halflings and English yeomen

"The Hobbits are, of course, really meant to be a branch of the specifically human race (not Elves or Dwarves)," Tolkien once wrote to his publisher. They are, however, "entirely without non-human powers, but are represented as being more in touch with 'nature'… and, abnormally for humans, free from ambition or greed of wealth. They are made *small*… partly to exhibit the pettiness of man, plain unimaginative, parochial man… and mostly to show up, in creatures of very small physical power, the amazing and unexpected heroism of ordinary men 'at a pinch'."

Compared to humans, Hobbits have extraordinary senses of hearing, sight, and smell. They are quick and nimble, and capable of seemingly disappearing into the landscape. Although Hobbits do not possess great physical strength, they are generally sturdily built and remarkably resilient to extreme rigours of the body. They enjoy dinner parties, picnics, large family celebrations, and anniversaries where they may dance, sing, debate genealogical histories, and recite silly poems. They are generally of cheerful disposition and healthy constitution, and commonly live for well over a century.

Sometimes known as Halflings, Hobbits are an elusive, curly-headed folk most easily distinguished by their diminutive size – between two and four feet in height – and their large, hairy feet. The horticultural skills of the Hobbits on their farms or in their orchards and gardens are legendary. They wear plain country clothing, but are prone to brightly coloured waistcoats. They are fond of drinking and smoking, and consume up to six meals a day. Although the Hobbits live in "holes" called "smials" (pronounced "smiles"), these are not dark or damp, but rather are warm, well-lit, wood-panelled, well-padded, well-stocked, and rather overfurnished dwellings of the most cheerful and homely sort.

The homeland of the Hobbits of Middle-earth was the tilled fields and farmlands of "The Shire". This was JRR Tolkien's romanticized analogy for the rural and pre-industrial English Shires of his late Victorian childhood. His Hobbits were the yeomen of England's "green and pleasant land". His Hobbits were to the tilled fields and rolling farmlands what Dwarves were to the mountains: the genii, or guardian spirits, of the place.

"'The Shire' is based on rural England and not any other country in the world," Tolkien once wrote. It was also: "a 'parody' of rural England, in much the same sense as are its inhabitants: they go together and are meant to. After all the book is English, and by an Englishman…"

Below The Shire, home of the Hobbits of Middle-earth is based on the countryside where Tolkien grew up, in the West Midlands of England. The whole Hobbit way of life was an affectionate and humorous representation of the English at large.

The first Hobbit

Curiously, we know exactly where and how that very first Hobbit made its appearance in Tolkien's mind. On a warm summer afternoon in 1930, JRR Tolkien sat at his desk in his study at 20 Northmoor Road in the suburbs of Oxford. He was engaged in the "everlasting weariness" of marking School Certificate papers, when "on a blank leaf I scrawled 'In a hole in the ground there lived a hobbit.' I did not and do not know why."

Tolkien was a professor of Anglo-Saxon and a philologist: a scholar who studies words and their origins. He had worked as a scholar on the *Oxford English Dictionary* and knew the English language (and a multitude of other languages) to its very roots. So when Tolkien later spoke of that moment when the word "hobbit" first came to him, he commented: "Names always generate a story in my mind. Eventually I thought I'd better find out what hobbits were like. But that was only a beginning." Indeed, "only a beginning" is a ridiculous understatement.

Tolkien really did start with the word "Hobbit". It became a kind of riddle that needed solving. He decided that he must begin by inventing a philological origin for the word "Hobbit" as a worn-down form of an original invented word "holbytla" (which is actually an Anglo-Saxon or Old English construct), meaning "hole builder". Therefore, the opening line of the novel is meant as an obscure lexicographical joke and a weird piece of circular thinking: "In a hole in the ground there lived a hole builder."

Tolkien, not content to joke in just one invented language, extends this to a series of philological puns on "hole" and "hole builder" in Old English, Old German ("hohl"), and an invented "Hobbitish" speech ("khuduk") based on constructs from extinct Gothic ("kûd-dûkan") and prehistoric German ("khulaz") words. (In later years, he would invent two variations in his Elvish language, another one in the language of the Dwarves, and several in the Mannish tongues.) This is an unusual way to develop a character and write a novel, but was clearly an essential part of Tolkien's creative process. Nearly all aspects of Hobbit life and adventure seem to evolve from names for people and things which themselves dictate the direction of the story. Names resonate with the force of their legends: words that name or describe dragons or demons often carry force over the human imagination even if their history is unknown and tale untold.

With this depth of background, it should not be so surprising that it took Tolkien six years to find out what that first Hobbit was like. In the seventh year, the rest of the world had its first opportunity to read the story about a Hobbit named Bilbo Baggins of Bag End and a Winged Fire-dragon named Smaug the Golden. *The Hobbit* was published in 1937 and rapidly established itself as a children's classic. It would take another 17 years, however, before Hobbits would be heard of again. This came with the publication of *The Lord of the Rings* in 1954.

Anglo-Saxons and Hobbits

Of course, once the word "Hobbit" had a history, then the history of the Hobbit race had to be "discovered" and chronicled by Tolkien. If Hobbits were meant to be quintessentially English, logic dictated that the ancient history of Hobbits and the Anglo-Saxons should have common ground. Consequently, Tolkien "discovered" that the origins of both peoples were lost in the mists of time beyond a distant and massive eastern range of mountains: the Alps for the Anglo-Saxons and the Misty Mountains for the Hobbits. Eventually, both races make mountain crossings and

settle for centuries in wedge-shaped delta regions called the Angle. Wars and invasions force both peoples to make water crossings and establish new homelands: the English Shires for Anglo-Saxons and The Shire for the Hobbits. Not so coincidentally, the names of the Anglo-Saxon and Hobbit founders are all linked by Old English words for "horse": Hengist (stallion) and Horsa (horse); Marcho (horse) and Blanco (white horse). This last stage of migration results in the division of each nation into three racial divisions. The three Anglo-Saxon tribes – the Saxons, Angles, and Jutes – are comparable to the three Hobbit breeds or strains – Harfoot, Fallohide, and Stoor.

Harfoots are the smallest and most typical Hobbits: the standard-issue diminutive, brown-skinned, curly-headed, hairy-footed, hole-dwelling Hobbit. The most numerous of the three, they are conservative in their habits and are the least adventurous, although they have been known to trade with Dwarves. Naturally gifted as farmers, they delight in the peace and quiet of country life.

Harfoot is a famous English surname, derived from the Old English "hare-foot", meaning "fast runner", or "nimble as a hare". Most celebrated was Harold Harefoot, who became one of the last Saxon kings, Harold I. The association of Hobbits with hares not only implies a nimble creature, but also one with keen eyes and ears, as well as oversized feet. Also, there is the implied pun "hair-foot" suggestive of a strange, hairy-footed creature capable of rapidly vanishing into the landscape. Thus we have in the "Har-Hare-Hair-Foot" composite creature a succinct description of this breed: a small, nimble creature with large, hairy feet. Typical Harfoot surnames names would be: Brown, Brownlock, Sandheaver, Tunnelly, Burrows, Gardner, Hayward, and Roper.

Fallohides are woodland dwellers in origin, the least numerous and the most unconventional of Hobbits. Usually the tallest and slimmest of Hobbits, they are commonly fair skinned, fair-haired, and the most likely to consort with Elves and go on adventures. Almost any display of individuality or ambition exhibited by normally conventional Hobbits is usually attributed to a distant Fallohide bloodline. Unfortunately for "normal" Hobbits, Fallohide blood seems to have produced the most distinguished and accomplished individuals in the annals of the Shire. The Fallohide breed's name is as descriptive as the others: "falo" is from Old High German, meaning "pale yellow" (as in the colour of a fallow deer), and "hide", as in skin or pelt; this is aptly descriptive of this yellow-haired and fair-skinned breed. "Fallow" is old English for "newly plowed land" and "hide" is an Old English measure of land sufficient for a household – and perhaps an ancient Hobbit unit as well. Typical fair-haired Fallohide family names are: Fairbairn, Goold, Goldworthy, Headstrong, and Boffin.

Left The three types of Hobbits, the Stoor (left), the Fallohide (centre), and the Harfoot (right) are roughly equivalent to the three tribes, the Jutes, the Angles, and the Saxons, who at various times invaded and settled in England.

Far left As a pipe-smoker himself, Tolkien has his Hobbits smoke the herb "Pipe-weed", to which the wizard Gandalf was also rather partial.

Stoors are the largest and strongest of Hobbits and the most like humans. The Stoors were the first Hobbits to live in houses, and they tend to live near rivers and marshes. They are also the only Hobbits to use footwear – usually Dwarf boots – and they are the only Hobbits capable of growing any kind of beard or facial hair. Stoors also distinguish themselves by being the only breed that is unafraid of water or even considers the idea of boating and swimming. Through their commerce on the river, the Stoors are among the wealthiest of Hobbits. The name "Stoor" appears to be appropriately derived from the Middle English "stur" and the Old English "stor", meaning "hard" or "strong". It also suggest "store", in the sense of being merchants, but even more in the sense that all Hobbits are hoarders with many storage spaces and rooms in their holes. Typical Stoorish names are: Banks, Puddifoot, Cotton, and Cotman.

Hobmen and hollow hills

Tolkien's Hobbits, naturally enough, relate to the traditions of the land itself. Hobbits are derived, in part, from creatures in the earliest British mythology. These are the Celtic sprites of the untamed British hills and forests: the brownies, who commonly were known as hobs, hobmen, hob thrusts, and hob hursts. These sprites were a diminutive, hairy, elusive race, mostly friendly towards humans. Brownies measured two to three feet in height and hid themselves away in the "hollow hills" (usually ancient grave mounds or barrow tombs) of the wild Celtic landscape.

It seems we do not have to look very far for direct inspiration for Tolkien's race of hole-dwelling little people. Hobs and hobmen were frequently called the "people of the hills". Tolkien certainly knew a great deal about the tales and traditions of the Celtic brownies. Indeed, only a few miles from Tolkien's Oxford home, there is an ancient round barrow tomb still known as Hob Hurst's House. Hobs and Tolkien's hobbits are, however, two very distinct races in nature and purpose. What Tolkien gives us in his tea-drinking, pipe-smoking, middle-class, home-and-garden-oriented Hobbits is a distinctively English transmutation of the rather wild and anything-but-middle-class hobs and hobmen of the Celts.

In fact, Tolkien's Hobbits are a distillation of all that is fundamentally "English", regardless of era. The anachronisms of the genteel "cakes and tea" manners of the late Victorians mixed with the tribal traditions of the ancient Anglo-Saxons are intentional and meant to be gently satirical. At the same time, there is a serious intent on Tolkien's part to create in his Hobbits a race that embodies the enduring spirit of that ideal "little England" characterized by the lands and villages of the English Shires.

Below Upon the return home of the heroic Hobbits after the War of the Ring, the Battle of Bywater and the subsequent scouring of The Shire cleansed the region of the evil servants of Saruman. Tolkien always strongly denied that this reflected events in England at the time of writing, during the Second World War.

Tolkien himself was a "little Englander" par excellence. He claimed to be essentiallly a Hobbit in all but height. His Shire was modelled on the rural West Midlands of his early childhood years which remained close to his heart. Tolkien wrote of the importance of his heritage both in his imaginative fiction and his academic work: "I am indeed in English terms a West Midlander at home only in the counties upon the Welsh Marches; and it is, I believe, as much due to descent as to opportunity that Anglo-Saxon and Western Middle English and alliterative verse have been both a childhood attraction and my main professional sphere."

Kings and Halflings

As *The Lord of the Rings* begins as fairy tale and evolves into legend and romance on an epic scale, so the smaller-than-life Hobbits themselves evolve into legendary heroes around whose deeds, Tolkien would have us believe, the heroic myths and romances of later times are woven.

In *The Lord of the Rings*, Frodo's adventures appear at first to be a foil to Aragorn's great deeds. The Hobbit is too frail and all too human to appear initially as a likely candidate for the role of questing hero. Aragorn is large, strong, bold, and almost inhuman in his fearlessness and virtue. In the end, however, it is the human qualities of compassion and humility in the Hobbit that are finally what are required to prevail in the quest. The deep wisdom of compassion found in the human (or Hobbit) heart succeeds where heroic strength cannot.

Strangely enough, in the chronicles of Middle-earth, it soon becomes apparent that the acts of greatest courage are achieved by its smallest protagonists. Time and time again, the Hobbits perform feats of great heroism or cunning, sometimes turning the tide of events, although this may not be apparent at the time. This can be seen in Meriadoc Brandybuck's role in the slaying of the Witch-King of Morgul. and Samwise Gamgee who mortally wounds the evil Giant Spider, Shelob, to give just two examples.

In the end, it is the humble Frodo Baggins, not the noble Aragorn, who achieves the Ring Quest. Frodo's moral courage is as remarkable as his endurance. It is not the High King of Middle-earth, but Frodo the Halfling who is chosen to sail in the Swan Ships beyond the spheres of the world to the Isle of Avallónë.

Ring-bearer and peacemaker

In the naming of things, Tolkien's creatures and places took on a life of their own. The names of all Tolkien's characters in some way shaped their personalities and destinies. One might look at the original Hobbit, Bilbo Baggins. Baggins was originally a Middle English Somerset surname, Bagg, meaning "money-bag" or "wealthy"; while "baggins" means "afternoon tea or snack between meals". Certainly, Baggins is an appropriate family name for a prosperous and well-fed Hobbit.

Our hero's first name suggests something very different. A bilbo is a rapier, or short, piercing sword, noted for the temper and elasticity of its blade. The word dates back to the mid-sixteenth century where it can be found as an earlier English form of the name "Bilbao", the Spanish town noted for the manufacture of fine blades. The name suggests the opposite of Baggins; this is something dangerous, bright like the Elf blade "Sting" that pierced Shelob's belly, or the sharp wit that proved fatal to Smaug the Golden. In these names, we have the contradictory character of the reluctant hero in the story of the Hobbit. Bilbo's heir to the Ring was Frodo, meaning "wise" – an apt name for this hero – while his servant was named Samwise, which actually carries the meaning "half-wise", or "simple".

Frodo the Wise was also an allusion to a literary figure of some importance to Tolkien. The deeper historical and mythical associations with Frodo obviously contributed to the character and the destiny of the Ring Bearer. In Old English and Norse mythology, the name Frodo (or Froda, Frothi, Frotha) is most often linked with the role of "peacemaker". In the Old English saga *Beowulf*, there is Froda the King of the Heathobards who attempts to make peace between the Danes and Bards. In Norse mythology, there is a King Frothi who rules a realm of peace and prosperity. Also, in Icelandic texts, we find the expression "Frotha-frith", meaning "Frothi's peace", with reference to a legendary "age of peace and wealth". This is in tune with Frodo's attempts to avoid bloodshed at the Battle of Bywater at the end of the War of the Ring. After the carnage of the war, Frodo the Wise became a respected counsellor and peacemaker throughout Middle-earth.

Certainly, within the Shire, Hobbits experienced the equivalent of the Norse legend of "Frotha-frith", or "Frodo's Peace", the year after the Battle of Bywater, in the time of the First Blossoming of the Golden Tree of Hobbiton. The war-ravaged Shire was transformed and filled with an Elvish enchantment. In that year, many children born to Hobbits were golden-haired and beautiful, and all prospered in the Shire. This became the "Year of Great Plenty" when the harvest was like a river of gold passing through the Shire. That year marked the beginning of a golden age of the Shire, the "Age of Peace and Wealth".

Yet, the concerns of Frodo the Wise were now beyond the affairs of the mortal world. It was the duty of his sturdy companion Samwise Gamgee to give counsel to the Hobbits of the Shire. Like his namesake Froda the Heathobard, Frodo Baggins passes from the sphere of the mortal world into the immortal realm of fairy tale and myth. Frodo the Ring Bearer has, through his heroism and suffering, achieved the status of the saviour of Middle-earth in Myth Time. Just as Tolkien's earlier hero

Eärendil the Mariner and the Saxon hero Earendel the Bright Angel are meant to be mythic forerunners of the historic prophet John the Baptist, so Tolkien's Hobbit hero Frodo the Ring Bearer and the Saxon hero Frothi the Peacemaker are meant to be mythic forerunners of that other historic Prince of Peace.

The Dominion of Wizards

Fairy-tale magicians and Istari

Gandalf the Wizard appears in *The Hobbit* as a standard fairy-tale character: a rather comic, eccentric fairy-tale magician in the company of a band of Dwarves. In *The Hobbit*, Gandalf the Grey has something of the character of the absent-minded history professor and muddled conjurer about him. Gandalf also fulfils the traditional role of mentor, adviser, and tour guide for the hero (or anti-hero) of the story. Wizards are extremely useful and versatile as vehicles for developing fairy-tale plots as their presence in so many tales testifies. Wizards usually provide a narrative with: a reluctant hero, secret maps, translations of ancient documents, supernatural weapons (how to use), some monsters (how to kill), location of treasure (how to steal), and an escape plan (negotiable).

Gandalf the Grey certainly fits into this tradition of the fairy tale. It is Gandalf who brings the Dwarves and the Hobbit together at the start of the story and sets them on their quest. It is his injection of adventure and magic into the mundane world of the Hobbits that transforms Bilbo Baggins's world. It is Gandalf who leads the band of outlaw adventurers in the form of Thorin and Company to Bilbo's door. And it is just this combination of the everyday and the epic that makes *The Hobbit* so compelling. Grand adventures with dragons, trolls, elves, and treasure are combined with the afternoon teas, toasted muffins, pints of ale, and smoke-ring-blowing contests.

So, in *The Hobbit*, Gandalf is a wandering fairy-tale magician with the standard traveller's cape, floppy boots, long walking staff, and traditional broad-brimmed pointed hat. He is an amusing and reassuring presence in the same way that an odd and distant uncle amuses everyone with charming firework displays and amateur card tricks at family parties. Gandalf's subsequent transformation into a grave and formidable figure in *The Lord of the Rings* is therefore something of a surprise. The force of his personality and his sense of purpose have increased tenfold in this world of high epic romance. Of course, this was the exact point Tolkien wanted made: fairy-tale magicians were simply domesticated versions of powerful archetypal Wizards. Consequently, in *The Lord of the Rings*, Tolkien reveals the "true tradition" and pedigree of the Wizards of Middle-earth. Although appearing as no more than a bearded traveller, Gandalf the Grey was one of the Istari, the ancient Order of Wizards. ("Istari" means "wizard"; and "wizard" means "wise man".) The Istari were a brotherhood who arrived on the western shores of Middle-earth in the Third Age.

Below We first meet Gandalf in *The Hobbit*, leading Bilbo, Thorin and Company on the Quest to the Lonely Mountain. He is a curious and eccentric fellow like the wizards in children's stories; by the time of *The Lord of the Rings*, he has evolved into a much more serious and awe-inspiring character.

In origin, the Istari were immortals who had lived for millennia in the Undying Lands. They were the angelic powers called the Maiar who were older than the World. Yet in the mortal lands of Middle-earth, they were forbidden to come forth in their immortal form. They were to become advisers to kings and stewards of mortal lands. There were five Istari in all, and they included Saruman the White, Sauron the Great, and of course, Gandalf the Grey.

In the name of the Wizard

As with most of Tolkien's creative works, names and language plays its part in the development of character and destiny. What can we discover in the name of the Wizard Gandalf? The meaning of the name Gandalf can be translated as "sorcerer elf". Looking at other elements, however, it is obvious that there are several ways of translating it. Its meaning shifts just about as much as the wizard's identity. Indeed, it is easy to see how the name Gandalf itself might have been used as the inspiration for the twist in the plot of *The Lord of the Rings*, wherein Gandalf the Grey is transformed into Gandalf the White.

Gandalf comes from the name "Gandalfr", listed in the ancient Old Icelandic Dvergata "Roll of the Dwarves". The Old Norse elements of Gandalfr are either "gand" and "alfr", or "gandr" and "alf". The last element of both, "alf" and "alfr" means either "elf" or "white". If the first element is "gand", it means a magical power, or the power of Gand, ie "astral travelling". Alternatively, the element is "gandr" which means an object used by sorcerers or an enchanted staff, or the enchanted crystal of a wizard. All elements resonate with aspects of wizardry and are suggestive of a collective meaning. As to direct translation of the name Gandalf, there are three fairly solid suggestions: "elf wizard", "white staff", and "white sorcerer". All three translations are admirably suitable names for a wizard. However, Tolkien would very likely argue that each translated aspect of this particular wizard had other definitions hidden within. The implications of these played a considerable part in shaping the fate of the character.

The translation of "elf wizard", applies descriptively because Gandalf is the Wizard most closely associated with the Grey Elves of Middle-earth. In addition, Gandalf had lived for ages among the Light Elves of Eldamar in the Undying Lands. Consequently, a story line suggesting the return of the Elf Sorcerer to the realm of the Light Elves could be implied. In fact, combining the two translations of "alf" with "sorcerer", there is a kind of confirmation of that plot with "white-elf wizard".

"White staff" is a strong name because the staff is the primary symbol by which a wizard is known. It symbolizes the ancient sceptre of power in disguise ("sceptre" being the Greek word for "staff") reduced by theatre magician's to a small wand. The translation of Gandalf as "white wizard" demonstrates precisely how influential the meaning hidden within a name could be for Tolkien. Initially Gandalf was given the title and rank of Grey Wizard, while Saruman was the White Wizard. We are told that Saruman the White Wizard's Elven name was Curunír, which means "Man of Skill" – a reasonable name for a white wizard. However, the name Saruman is an Old English construct meaning "Man of Pain", a name which could only be given to an evil (black) wizard. Similarly, we are told that Gandalf the Grey Wizard's Elven name was Mithrandir, which means "Grey-wanderer" – an apt name for a grey wizard. As we have seen, however, the name Gandalf is an Old Norse construct meaning "white sorcerer", a name that could only be given to a good (white) wizard.

As we have come to appreciate, the hidden meaning of names often predicts the fate of Tolkien's characters: Saruman the White Wizard became the evil sorcerer of Isengard, while Gandalf the Grey was reincarnated as Gandalf the White Wizard. Once again, Tolkien is acting the part of a magician and has set us up for a conjurer's trick with language: a little verbal manipulation wherein white becomes black, and grey becomes white.

Finally, it seems that Tolkien might have been inspired to make one final link between his two Wizards' fates through contemplating a couple of alternative translations of the first element in Gandalf's name: "gandr" as "an enchanted crystal" and "gand" as "astral travelling". Remarkably enough, we find that Saruman's downfall comes through his misuse of an enchanted crystal called a "Palantir", while the salvation of Gandalf comes through a form of "astral travelling" that permitted his resurrection after falling with the Balrog from the Bridge of Moria. As Gandalf the White, the Wizard offered no explanation for his resurrection. He simply replied: "I strayed out of thought and time." It is, perhaps, the best definition possible for "astral travelling" or possibly for that mysterious thing we can now only know as the "power of Gand".

Wizard of the White Hand

By no means everything in Tolkien's black-and-white universe was fixed as either "black" or "white." Such rigidity would have prevented much exploration of character and development of the story. The most significant case in point is that of Saruman, who at the beginning of *The Lord of the Rings* is represented as one of the forces of good; indeed head of the White Council of wizards. At first, Gandalf himself has no doubts of Saruman's virtue and good intentions. Eventually it becomes all too clear that Saruman, for all his gifts, has allowed himself to be corrupted. Power, the great seducer, has affected even him. Tolkien was very conscious of power and of the responsibility and self-discipline that ought to go with

Above The evil wizard Saruman meets a grisly death at the hands of his former accomplice Gríma Wormtongue. The moral is twofold; that greed for power can corrupt the good, and that by attracting people as treacherous as yourself you are likely to be betrayed.

it. His most admirable characters, such as Aragorn and Faramir, wear their power lightly, or keep it cloaked. On occasion, some of his main protagonists are momentarily tempted to show their powers at full manifestation: the celebrated scene between Frodo and Galadriel is the best example. She knows it to be a test, and she passes, but not without expressing a tinge of regret. It is by a surrendering of power that the Elves leave Middle-earth, to its loss. Saruman fails the test; his freedom to choose has led him in the wrong direction. But then of course, Power is the mainspring of the whole saga: it is the potency of the One Ring that sets all the events in motion.

Interestingly, in *The Lord of the Rings*, there is a connection between towers, their inhabitants, and power. Three great towers, three lords. One, the mightiest, the lord of Barad-dûr, is already and wholly committed to evil – the dominion and degradation of every living thing. Another, Saruman, lord of Isengard, has taken the first insidious steps in that same direction. The third, Denethor, Steward of Minas Tirith, is a man. He is not a wicked figure; in many ways he is portrayed as noble. But he too has been beguiled by the appearance of power, and has become arrogant and short-sighted in his long exercising of supreme authority in Gondor. By contrast, Gandalf, not the least powerful of the protagonists, does not even have a home. He is a wanderer, the Grey Pilgrim. There is some food for thought here, though Tolkien was probably not consciously making a point. As in other great stories, many themes and ideas emerge by accident, or coincidentally. Much can, of course, also be read into the story, and links and connections descried which the author quite possibly never considered or intended.

Tolkien was quite clear, however, on the links between petty tyranny, exploitation and bullying, and the cosmic evil of a figure such as Melkor. When Saruman is defeated and ruined as a wizard, and deprived of his supernatural powers, he retains an ability to dominate, hurt and destroy. And the author allows him to inflict it on the place nearest to his own heart, the Shire, where the happy parody of Merrie England rapidly becomes a kind of Blakean nightmare of pollution, oppression, collaboration with the enemy, passive resistance and punishment. Tolkien always denied any direct correspondence between his own world and what was happening in the course of the 1930s and the Second World War; and as we have seen, his creative attention was often focused thousands of years earlier. In a sense, real events were mirroring those of his creative imagination. The ruining of the Shire is as intrinsic to his story as any other episode.

Wandering gods – Hermes and Mercury

The most common portrayal of the Wizard is that of a solitary wanderer wearing a broad-brimmed hat and a long traveller's cape, and bearing a long staff. Traditionally, these wanderers tend to be bearded and world-weary individuals of distant or unknown origin. They are often mesmerizing when it comes to the telling of tales and recitation of literature, but they are "outsiders". They do not appear to have any personal wealth or material support; they do not have definable status or social position; nor do they have families or homes. Literate in many languages and customs, these solitary wanderers are widely believed to be capable of casting spells and curses, and of acts of sorcery.

What is seldom observed about the wizard's garb is that it was the same costume worn by nearly all pilgrims and professional travellers in antiquity. There were many peripatetic professions and activities: travelling scholars, pilgrims, traders, merchants, scribes, surveyors, musicians, conjurers, and apothecaries, all of whom dressed in similar garb. There were also professional messengers, couriers, and diplomatic envoys who were continuously on the road, and they wore stylized "uniform" versions of the same costume.

This was probably because it was a combination of clothing that was best suited to travelling in all weathers. It is also how the Greek god Hermes (the Roman god Mercury) was portrayed in his guise as the god of travellers. Hermes was also the swift messenger of the gods, and a pillar featuring this bearded god of travellers appeared at most crossroads. As Hermes, like his fellow god Odin, frequently appeared on Earth as an ordinary traveller, both civic law and popular superstition supported the traditions of hospitality —as any traveller might be a god in disguise, so they should be treated.

It therefore did no harm to a poor pilgrim to somewhat resemble this god of travellers, who was also the god of magicians, alchemists, merchants, pilgrims, scholars, messengers, envoys, diplomats, and – predictably – liars and thieves. As the herald of the gods, Hermes (or Mercury) passes through all the domains of the other gods: from Zeus (or Jupiter) up high on Olympus, where he is the herald of the gods, to Hades (or Pluto) in the Underworld, where he guides the souls of the dead.

It may be supposed that when the ancients decided to assign gods and their influences to the planets, Mercury as the Grey-wanderer (and speeding messenger) must have been one of their more obvious choices. After all, the word "planet" is Greek for "wanderer". (As most stars are "fixed" in the sky, the most obvious quality of a planet is its ability to wander through the night sky, hence the use of this word for this particular meaning.) Mercury is observably a silver-grey "wanderer" travelling at phenomenal speed across the night sky, visiting each god or planet, as their paths cross. There could be no clearer case for matching up the mercurial nature of both the planet and the god.

Odin – god of shamanic wizards

Ancient Greek and Roman writers and diarists who personally encountered German and Norse tribes were unanimous in their belief that Odin was identical to their own Hermes (or, in the case of the Romans, Mercury). This was certainly true of the manifestations of both deities in the wizard-god's Grey-wanderer aspects. Almost all that can be said about Hermes can equally be applied to Odin and his travels in the mortal world.

Hermes' father was the god Zeus, and his mother was the Titan Earth spirit whose name is Maia. Gandalf in his origin was of similar status, originating from the demi-gods of Tolkien's Maiar race. Even more curiously, Maia was a queen of woodlands, and her people were nymphs and sylphs, naiads and dryads. The oldest of these nature spirits were the Melias, who were the spirits who lived in the ash trees (or perhaps they were the spirit of the ash Yggdrasil the World Tree). They appear to have been somewhat like the Entwives; however, names of the titan and the spirit suggest another entity: Melian the Maia, Queen of the Grey Elves.

Odin was much closer to his shamanic roots than most of the wizards and gods. The shaman is a magician, mystic, healer, and poet. He travels between the

world of men and the worlds of spirits and animals, and even into the land of the dead. He makes his ascent or descent by going into a trance and then being carried by an animal familiar.

Like Hermes, Odin was a great traveller and seeker of wisdom. He travelled the Nine Worlds asking questions of every living thing: giants, elves, dwarfs, and spirits. He questioned the trees, plants, and the very stones themselves. Odin often endured many trials and dangerous adventures, but from each he wrung what wisdom there was from all things he encountered and gained more power. He was a god, poet, sorcerer, warrior, trickster, transformer, necromancer, mystic, and ultimately a shaman-king.

His method of travel was part of this tradition and required ecstatic frenzy to drive the soul through a kind of grey limbo between worlds. That is why we have the Grey Travellers, the Grey Havens, and the Grey Horses. Gandalf the Grey has chosen the horse called "Shadowfax", meaning "silver-grey", which closely resembles "Grani the Grey", the steed of Sigurd who was Odin's champion in *The Volsunga Saga*. Grani, who – like Shadowfax – understood human speech, was the silver-grey offspring of Odin's supernatural eight-legged horse, Sleipnir. And it was on Sleipnir that Odin road down through the Nine Worlds.

Grey is the pathway between worlds. Once again, we come back to both the silver-grey planet that is Mercury and the silver-grey metal. The world of Hermes is also a world of secrets. The alchemists named the liquid metal quicksilver after Mercury. As the god Hermes was known for his diplomatic silence, the term "hermetic" came to mean "sealed" or "secret". Consequently, alchemy came to be known as the hermetic science. All these wizards, these grey pilgrims, are guardians of this arcane wisdom.

Mentors – Merlin and Gandalf

In Arthurian romance, Merlin is the greatest of all wizards. He is the future king's mentor, adviser, and chief strategist in both peace and war. He is also the presiding intelligence and organizing principle in Camelot. He is its supernatural protector. Merlin is immortal, but has mortal emotions and empathy. He is an enchanter who communes with spirits of woods, mountains, and lakes, and has tested his powers in duels with other wizards and enchantresses.

To many, it appeared that just as Merlin was the chief counsellor of King Arthur, the future King of the United Kingdom, in his court of Camelot, so it seemed that it was Gandalf who played this role for Aragorn II, the future King of the Reunited Kingdom of the Dúnedain people.

Although the archetypal figures of hero and wizard are clearly similar in pagan saga, medieval legend, and modern fantasy, the context in each is clearly different. The Christian moral principles of Arthurian romance are quite different to the Norse tradition of Odin and Sigurd. Curiously, although Tolkien's world is a pagan, pre-religious one, his hero, Aragorn, has strict views on absolute good and evil. Aragorn may be a pagan hero, but he is even more upright and moral than the Christian King Arthur.

Merlin and Gandalf are both travellers of great learning, with long, white beards and who carry a staff and wear broad-brimmed hats and long robes. They are both non-human beings. Both are counsellors for future kings in peace and war, yet they have no interest in worldly power themselves.

The deaths and passing of Merlin and Arthur are directly linked to that of Gandalf and Aragorn. The Last Sailing of the Keepers of the Rings is heavily redolent of Arthurian romantic traditions, but the roles are reversed. Merlin and Aragorn are laid to rest in mortal lands, while Gandalf and Arthur sail off with the Elven Queen to the immortal isle of Avallónë, or Avalon.

Once known as Merlin the Wild, Merlin the Wizard has become less the Grey-wanderer and more Merlin the Architect of Camelot and the strategist who creates rational order. Gandalf's concern is for the descendants of the Dúnedain household and the Reunited Kingdoms of the North and South Kingdoms of Arnor and Gondor. As mentor to Aragorn II, who is to become the future King Elessar of the Reunited Kingdom, Gandalf is duplicating exactly the role of the wizard Merlin as the mentor of the future King Arthur. He is also duplicating the role of Charlemagne's mentor, the English scholar or priest Alcuin, as the architect of the Holy Roman Empire.

This is a fundamental difference between the Norse Midgard and Tolkien's Middle-earth. The Norse mythic world is essentially amoral, while Tolkien's world is consumed by the great struggle between the forces of good and evil. The entire epic tale of *The Lord of the Rings* is in part about the struggle for the control of the world by these conflicting powers, as embodied in the duel between the white Wizard and the black Wizard.

Ringwraiths and the Witch-king

The Black Riders

In his creation of the malignant and terrifying Nazgûl, the greatest of the servants of Sauron, Tolkien taps into rich lodes of mythology and legend. Rings have a long history and a variety of symbolic meanings. Invisibility is associated with them, as in Luned's ring, worn by Owain in Arthurian legend; and Otnit's Ring of Invisibility in the old tales of the Lombards; again in the Arthurian stories, the Ring of Ogier confers the gift of youth and health. Thus the properties of the Nazgûl rings, which hide and preserve them even in their "undead" form, are attested from European culture-memory – Tolkien, of course, would have it the other way round: the memory of the Rings of Middle-earth eventually found a place as the basis of later tales.

The wraith is a phantom or spectre, either a manifestation of a living being; or the ghost of a dead person. In English it is a relatively recent word, first noted around 1513, but the notion it conveys is of vastly greater antiquity than the English language. For humans, the primal mysteries are birth and death, and of the two, death is much the harder to deal with and comprehend. Fear of the dead is a powerful force in many cultures. For the dead to return is almost invariably a cause of evil and disaster. Tolkien's Ringwraiths have something in common with the zombi – the mindless reanimated corpse set in motion by a voodoo sorceror, but he has created beings far more potent and malevolent than these spirits of the cane-field. Not only are they possessed by the will of Sauron, they were themselves sorcerors and kings of great power. They have the terror and grisly grandeur of the Four Horsemen of the Apocalypse, as well as the secret menace of walking Death, his skull-face hidden in his hood.

It was a stroke of genius to link these fearful beings of older legend with those phobic monsters of more modern times, the great winged lizards. Cold bloodedness, cruelty, rending claws – the nightmare combination has a compelling quality. And the literary tradition continues to this day. Echoes of the hunting, inexorable Nazgûl arise in the portrayal of the Dementors, in the "Harry Potter" novels of JK Rowling. More limited in their parts and powers, they exude the same sense of dread and the ability to destroy not only life but the living soul.

The curse of the Rings

It is Frodo who sees what the Nazgûl really look like at Weathertop, in the first book of *The Fellowship of the Ring*. Slipping the One Ring on his finger, he suddenly sees

Above These prehistoric, dinosaur-like winged creatures, even more ancient than dragons, were the fearsome steeds of the nine Ringwraiths during The War of the Ring.

Previous page In his depiction of the Black Riders, once great kings now corrupted, Tolkien echoes other mythical traditions of Dark Knights, as expressed, for example, in Keats' poem *La Belle Dame sans Merci*.

their white faces; their grey hair; long, grey robes; and "helms of silver". In some ways, they are not unlike the characters in the Keats poem *La Belle Dame Sans Merci*, a host of men seduced and enslaved by the "beautiful woman without mercy" – "Pale kings and princes, too, Pale warriors, death-pale were they all". The kings and sorcerers who make up the Nazgûl have similarly been seduced. Rather than the charms of a beautiful woman, however, it is the thought of riches and power that has ensnared them – at the terrible cost of selling their souls. As such, Tolkien is tapping into a rich mythological tradition: stories of powerful rings and the corrupting effect on those who wear them.

One example of this is in the famous ring legend of the Norsemen, *The Volsunga Saga*. Here the magic ring is known as the "Andvarinaut", originally belonging to the dwarf Andvari. Its name means "Andvari's loom" because it "wove" its owner a fortune in gold. In *The Volsunga Saga*, when Loki takes the ring from Andvari, the dwarf screams: "I curse you for this! The ring and the treasure it spawned will carry my curse forever. All who possess the ring and its treasure for long will be destroyed!" When Loki uses the ring and Andvari's gold to pay off the magician-king Hreidmar, it is Hreidmar's son Fafnir who is tempted by it. He kills his father to claim the ring and the gold, dragging it to a cavern under a mountain. Brooding over his treasure, his heart and mind are slowly poisoned, and his outward body, too, begins to match his inner evil. He becomes a serpent, a huge dragon – a creature whom Sigurd the Dragonslayer is later challenged to kill.

There is also resonance with the tale of the "Serpent's Ring" in the Carolingian Ring Legends. Among the presents on Charlemagne and Frastrada's wedding day is a great serpent with a gold ring in its mouth. Charlemagne puts the ring on Frastrada's finger, but soon it is he who is under its spell. The ring is one of enchantment, and Charlemagne is irrevocably bound to love and cherish whoever wears the ring. When Frastrada becomes ill and dies, Charlemagne refuses to leave her side and watches over her body day and night. Wasting away, neglecting his empire, Charlemagne's life is slowly being destroyed by the ring. It is only Bishop Turpin, who, like Gandalf and the One Ring, in his wisdom realizes the power of the Serpent's Ring and removes it.

Another ring worth mention is that of Draupnir, the ring of the Viking god Odin. Draupnir means "the dripper", and this magical ring has the power to drip eight other rings of equal size every nine days. Through Draupnir, Odin rules Asgard and uses the other eight rings as gifts of wealth and power by which the other eight worlds are governed. Just as Sauron hands out his Rings of Power to sorcerers and kings, so Odin gives his rings to chosen kings and heroes.

We should not overlook the fact that the Ringwraiths number nine. In Norse mythology, nine is by far the most significant number, from its nine worlds to the nine nights hanging on the World Tree, the great religious ceremonies at Uppsala lasting nine days in every ninth year, and so forth. Nine is the last of the series of single numbers, and, as such, in Norse mythology and others, it is seen as symbolizing both death and rebirth. Considering the payment of their souls for their Rings, and the "death" of the Men and their "rebirth" as Ringwraiths, the importance of the Nazgûl numbering nine should not be forgotten.

The Witch-king

The method by which Tolkien exalts his Dark Lord to the pinnacle of malevolent dominion is of interest. Though authority and decision rest only with the sleepless Sauron himself, a hierarchy of command rises from Orc-captains and fortress commanders to such figures as the "Mouth of Sauron" and Gothmog, lieutenant of Morgul. But his supreme servants are the Nazgûl, and supreme among them is the one-time Witch-king of Angmar. The Ring-Lord took counsel with nobody, and the Witch-king is chief servant rather than trusted adviser. (Here, incidentally, another weakness of the evil spirit is identified. While those who fight on the side of right can discuss policy, and exercise mutual trust, Sauron can trust no-one). The Nazgûl are consequently more like a specialized hit-squad, who can be placed, singly or together,

Above Never popular birds in rural England, Tolkien portrays the crows of Middle-earth as the carrion-eating black spies of Sauron. In effect, they can be seen as more numerous though less powerful manifestations of the Nazgûl, as they too traverse the skies of Middle-earth hunting the enemies of their overlord.

where their master feels the need; and who carry out his most crucial assignments. In the description of their terror, that of their controller is magnified.

The leader of the Nine Riders is distinguished by an individual role in the narrative. In the Battle of the Pelennor Fields, it is he who stoops to kill Théoden, king of Rohan, and meets his own death at the hand of Éowyn, disguised as a male rider. Dark irony thus cloaks his death, for, as he boasts, a prophecy has said that no man could kill him. Tolkien here picks up another familiar theme from ancient literature: the misinterpreted oracle. King Philip of Macedon, about to invade Persia, asked the Delphic Oracle if he would succeed. Its answer was:

"The ready victim crowned for death

Before the altar stands."

King Philip took it as an affirmation of his impending victory; but the victim proved to be himself.

There are two main figures that Tolkien draws on for the story of the Witch-king. The first is found within the medieval German romance tale that most resembles the imaginative sweep and dramatic impact of *The Lord of the Rings* – the tale of the hero Dietrich von Berne and Virginal, the Ice Queen of Jeraspunt. It is in this tale that we come across the evil Janibus the Necromancer, a character Tolkien used elements of for both the Witch-king and Sauron himself. The Ostrogoth Dietrich von Berne is based on the sixth-century Roman Emperor Theodoric the Goth. From his youth, Tolkien was enthralled with his most ancient ancestors: the Goths. While still at school, he discovered the Gothic language quite by chance, and in it "the acute aesthetic pleasure derived from a language for its own sake". He felt that surviving fragments of Gothic text combined with reading in Latin gave insights into an authentic ancient German culture. Remarkably, it was thanks to the Theodoric the Goth and his court that much of what remains of Gothic literature survived at all.

The tale of Dietrich and the Ice Queen begins with the hero entering the realm of a race of mountain giants ruled over by Orkise, the cannibal giant, and his evil son, Janibas the Wizard. Dietrich learns that the giants were making war on the highest mountain kingdom of the Ice Faeries in the snow-peaked Alps. This was the domain of the magical snow maidens who were ruled by Virginal, the Ice Queen, from her glittering Castle of Jeraspunt, on the highest peak in the Alps. Dietrich carries out a long campaign of war on the mountain giants, and, in one titanic battle, he meets and kills the terrible Giant Orkise himself. When he arrives within sight of the Ice Castle, however, he finds the way barred by the son of the giant king – a foe more formidable than Orkise himself. Janibas the Wizard has laid siege to the shining castle with an awesome army of giants, evil men, and monsters. To his foes, Janibas appears as a phantom Black Rider who commands tempests and is backed by

demons and hell-hounds. The wizard's most terrifying power, however, is his ability to command those who were slain in battle to rise up from the dead and fight again.

Dietrich can see the siege army lying like a black sea around the many-towered Ice Castle. It is obvious that, however well defended, the castle must eventually fall to the never-dwindling numbers of the sorcerer's army. Despite what would seem an impossible task, Dietrich is spurred to a battle frenzy by the sight of the beautiful Ice Queen on the battlements of the tallest tower. Her radiance matches even that of the star-like jewel dancing in her crown.

In his valiant attempt to raise the siege, Dietrich slaughters all before him, but this proves futile as the slain simply rise up to fight again. Seeing that Janibas commands his forces by means of a sorcerer's iron tablet held aloft, Dietrich pursues the Black Horseman himself. Striking Janibas down from his phantom steed, Dietrich lifts his sword and smashes the iron tablet. As the tablet breaks, the glaciers of the mountains split and shatter, thundering down in massive avalanches and burying the entire evil host of giants, phantoms, and undead forever. Dietrich triumphantly makes his way to the castle as the gates are flung open to greet him. He is welcomed by the incomparable Ice Queen herself, who is surrounded by her dazzling court of snow maidens, all aglow with fairy light and the glitter of their diamond veils.

In the legend of the Ice Queen, Janibas the Necromancer as the Black Horseman is like a combination of Sauron the Necromancer and his chief lieutenant, the Witch-king, lord of the Ringwraiths. The One Ring is replaced by an iron tablet, but the climax of the tale reads very like Sauron's ultimate battle at the Black Gate at the end of *The Lord of the Rings*. The effect of the destruction of the iron tablet on Janibas' evil legions is identical to the impact of the destruction of the One Ring on those of Sauron.

Perhaps Tolkien's greatest inspiration for the Witch-king, however, is a negative one: William Shakespeare's *Macbeth*. Tolkien profoundly disliked the play, although he was fascinated with its historic and mythic story. Not only did he enjoy voicing the ultimate Englishman's heresy of hating Shakespeare altogether, but also he voiced his dismissal of drama as a form a literature at all. Tolkien suggested that "disbelief had not so much to be suspended as hanged, drawn, and quarterted".

In his essay collection *On Fairy-Stories* Tolkien briskly informs us that, in the case of the legendary warrior, "Macbeth is indeed a work by a playwright who ought, at least on this occasion, to have written a story, if he had the skill or patience for that art." As Shakespeare was no longer available, Tolkien decided to take on the job himself. In his Lord of the Ringwraiths, we have a mortal man who has sold his immortal soul to Sauron for a ring of power and the illusion of earthly dominion. This tragedy, set within the context of his epic fantasy novel, is meant to suggest a grand and ancient archetype for *Macbeth*'s tale of a king who has lost his doomed and blasted soul.

So that none will mistake the comparison, or Tolkien's challenge to Shakespeare, the life of the Witch-king is protected by a prophecy that is almost identical to the final one that safeguards Macbeth. Tolkien's Witch-king "cannot be slain by the hand of man", while the similarly deluded Macbeth "cannot be slain by man of woman born". Tolkien's challenge to Shakespeare here concerns what he considers a pretty weak fulfillment of this prophecy. Certainly, in terms of a convincing plot, one must acknowledge that the Witch-king's death by a Hobbit and a woman disguised as a warrior is preferable to Shakespeare's loophole that someone born by Caesarean section is not, strictly speaking, "of woman born".

Barrow-wights and Phantoms

Tombs and dead men's gold

Belief in haunted tombs and the cursed treasures of the dead must surely be among the oldest of superstitions. Truly blood-curdling curses – meant as a deterrent to grave robbers – have been discovered written on the walls of Egyptian tombs. Judging from the widely held belief that the Curse of Tutankhamen was behind the deaths of many of the tomb's excavators, one can conclude that this must be one of the most persistent of superstitions.

It is also one of the most widespread. Examples can be drawn from a multitude of cultures, from Egypt to China to Mexico. It was especially significant among the Anglo-Saxons who, not unlike the ancient Egyptians had elaborate customs concerning the burial of their dead. After all, it is the disturbance of a barrow grave that leads directly to the death of the greatest hero in Anglo-Saxon literature. It was just Beowulf's bad luck that the guardian of this particular barrow happened to be a fire-breathing dragon.

In *The Lord of the Rings*, early on in their journey, the Hobbits enter the ancient burial grounds of the Barrow-downs, which were haunted by the Barrow-wights, tortured spirits of the victims of the Witch-king of Angmar. These burial mounds were raised in celebration of ancient kings, rather akin to similar earthworks seen in historic northern Europe. Barrow-wights were not an original Tolkien creation – they already had a long history, especially in the sagas of the Norsemen. These Norse tales tell of encounters similar to those experienced by the Hobbits. Most often the victims were unwary travellers held captive by evil spirits with terrifying luminous eyes and hypnotic voices. A skeletal hand would paralyze the body with a grip as cold as ice and as strong as steel. Once under the spell of the Barrow-wight, the victim has no will of his own. In this way, the Barrow-wight seems to have performed certain sacrificial rituals upon their victims before attempting to execute the final bloody sacrificial service with a sword.

Sutton Hoo and Wayland's Barrow

Monumental earthworks, stone circles, and barrow graves were often the focus of folk tales and legends relating to the ancestors of the English people. Some of these stories have survived as myths or fairy tales. As the only substantial monuments built by the early Anglo-Saxons, barrow graves and tombs were immediately looked to by archaeologists in the hope of discovering artefacts of this little-known and long-under-estimated culture. Unfortunately, barrow grave excavations produced few

Left Early in their adventure the Hobbits are captured by a Barrow-wight, a ghostly figure closely based upon the folk-tales of England surrounding supposedly haunted ancient burial mounds.

artefacts of great significance. All that changed, however, in the years immediately before the outbreak of the Second World War.

At a time when JRR Tolkien had just written the opening chapters of *The Lord of the Rings*, archeologists made an extraordinary discovery in Suffolk. Three Anglo-Saxon long barrow graves had been excavated at a site called Sutton Hoo. It was to be the historic equivalent of the Barrow-downs of Middle-earth. Sutton Hoo is the largest and oldest-surviving Anglo-Saxon burial ground in existence. Covering more than four hectares (10 acres), its barrows and tombs had been a burial ground for nearly three millennia.

Of the first three barrows opened at that time, the largest measured 36.5m (120ft) and 3.7m (12ft) high and contained a 27.4m (90ft) long ship – larger than any previously known ship of the time. It also revealed the richest-ever treasure trove of the Anglo-Saxon culture. The Sutton Hoo revelation of the ancient German world was as important as the discovery of Tutankhamen's tomb had been to our understanding of the ancient Egyptian world.

Tolkien does not appear to have visited Sutton Hoo, but we know he was familiar with many other long barrow gravesites. One was a particularly impressive barrow about 32km (20 miles) from Oxford called Wayland's Smithy. Wayland the Smith is manifest in Tolkien's world in the figure of Telchar the Dwarf-smith, who forged the blade of Narsil. Both were master swordsmiths who forged weapons with charmed blades that could cleave stone and flicker with a living flame.

This figure of the master-smith may be found in most German Romances and Norse sagas, as Wayland forged the swords for the majority of these heroes. One specific Norse saga, however, is of particular interest because its chief concern is with Wayland's Smithy.

In Thorsten's Saga, we are told that the daring pirate Sote the Outlaw broke into Wayland's barrow and found the treasure chamber filled with drifts of gold and gems. Yet something compelled him to pick up just one gold ring and place it on his hand. Within the tombs and passages of the barrow, and without realizing it, Sote the Outlaw thus became wed to the darkness.

Always fearful of the thieves who would seize either ring or treasure, Sote the Outlaw remains within the barrow. With drawn sword and dagger, the Outlaw is the never-sleeping guardian who endlessly stalks the corridors and chambers of Wayland's tomb. This is the curse and the power of Wayland's Ring: Sote becomes possessed by his possession. The ring is now his first, his last, his everything. Instead of looting the barrow, the Outlaw is forever condemned to the dark. Sote the Outlaw has become the haunting demon and guardian of treasure and tomb: the blasted spirit of the Barrow-wight.

Apart from being yet another example of the overwhelming power of these magic rings, in Sote the Barrow-wight, we see a likely source for the Hobbits' near-fatal encounter with the Barrow-wight in the early stages of the Ring Quest. In Tolkien's story, it is that peculiar spirit, Tom Bombadil, who effortlessly scatters the bones of the Barrow-wight and rescues the four novice adventurers. In the Norse version of the tale, however, the approach is more brutal and less humorous. Unlike the bizarre but wise Tom Bombadil, the Viking Thorsten is not immune to the terror and murderous intent of the Barrow-wight. Thorsten knows he must pay a price for his challenge, and there is nothing of Bombadil's comic exorcism in his actions. Thorsten simply depends on his vast strength of body and his unquenchable spirit. The Viking descends into the passages beneath the barrow. We soon hear the wailing screams of a tortured fiend, the cries of a living man. There is the sound of steel

striking stone and bone, and the flickering of sorcerous flames can be seen within. Finally, however, Thorsten emerges from the barrow as pale and bloody as a ghost, but in his hand is the glint of the gold ring.

Above The standing stones and barrows of the landscape through which the four Hobbits travel would fit seamlessly into any panorama of Anglo-Saxon England.

Gollum and the Ghouls

Beowulf's Gollum and Bilbo's Grendel

As Tolkien acknowledged, a great deal of the Anglo-Saxon epic poem *Beowulf* found its way into *The Hobbit*. One might easily argue that *The Hobbit* is a fairy-tale version of the epic reduced to it most elemental form. So what scaled-down monster was Gollum replacing in this fairy-tale version of *Beowulf*? Quite clearly, Gollum was to become a miniature version of Beowulf's monster, Grendel. By some evil power, the Ogre Grendel was granted supernatural strength and protection from attack by the weapons of his enemies. The monster came by night and murdered scores of warriors as they slept. It then broke their bones and consumed their flesh "like a wolf might eat a rabbit". Grendel was even feared by the walking-corpses and blood-sucking man-beasts that haunted the foul serpent-infested mere that he had made his home.

Although a diminished version of Grendel the Ogre, Gollum was no less a terror to his less celebrated victims, such as the Goblins (the fairy-tale name for Tolkien's demonic Orcs) and the Hobbit Bilbo Baggins. For, just as some unknown power gave Grendel enormous physical strength and long life, so the evil power of the Ring lengthened Gollum's miserable life for centuries and seemingly enhanced the power of his wraith-like hands, giving them murderous power to strangle his prey. Curiously, in the Anglo-Saxon epic, it is the hero, Beowulf, who is said to have a grip "equal to that of thirty men".

Both monsters are subhuman grotesques in appearance and habit. Gollum lived in the dank pools of dark caverns where he became thin and hairless. His eyes became bulbous, his feet webbed, and his teeth grew long and sharp through living off raw, unclean meat.

The monster Grendel had a similarly damned existence: he seems to have had little or no human speech. His nocturnal life was largely occupied with such activities as nightcrawling, cannibalism, and murder. Daylight hours seem to have been spent sleeping in a murky cave at the bottom of a filthy mere in the midst of a haunted wetland, not unlike the Dead Marshes of Middle-earth. Surrounded by his treasure and trophy weapons stolen from murdered men, the creature lived only to feed on human flesh. He was finally put out of his miserable existence when Beowulf used his powerful grip to tear off the monster's arm as they were engaged in combat. Finally, Beowulf followed Grendel's bloody trail to his cave on the bottom of the mere. No quarter was given in the ensuing battle, and Beowulf eventually slew the cowering, wounded monster.

Hobgoblins and Sméagol-Gollum

In Tolkien's novels, with the Hobbit and the Goblin we have diminutive, hole-dwelling races that embody the struggle between the forces of good and evil. "Hobgoblin" is the magic word that imaginatively links Hobbit with Goblin, but there was at least one other link that shows the reader that, creatively, Hobbit and Goblin emerged from the same hole.

The hobgoblin was critical to the evolution of the Hobbit as a species, and to the development of *The Hobbit* as a novel. Hobbit is a diminutive form of the root word "hob". Hobgoblin is a composite word: "hob' – a benevolent spirit, "goblin" – an evil spirit. The resulting hobgoblin is usually a mischievous creature, either a rather warped good spirit or a somewhat redeemed evil spirit. Either way, the hobgoblin was an ambivalent creature, not evil but frequently at odds with a human sense of right and wrong. More importantly, the hobgoblin is a paradoxical creature that provided a creative spark and fired Tolkien's imagination in the creation of several of the characters and nations of Middle-earth.

The dual nature of hobgoblins was also evident in the individual characters of Bilbo Baggins and Gollum. Gandalf the Wizard discovered that Gollum was, in

Below Gollum leads the Ring-bearer and his companion through the Dead Marshes where Tolkien continues the idea of ghostly manifestations seen earlier in the Barrow-wights, by infesting this swampland with the phantoms of dead warriors of a past age.

origin, an early strain of Hobbit from the Vales of Anduin. He was called Sméagol, and that name largely defined his nature. Sméagol comes from an Anglo-Saxon root meaning "burrowing, worming in". Consequently, Sméagol was said to possess a restless, inquiring nature. He was always searching and digging among the roots of things – constantly burrowing, but also twisting and turning, this way and that. Sméagol lived east of the Misty Mountains in the ancient, ancestral river valley homeland of the Stoorish Hobbits. Sméagol often fished and explored with his cousin and dearest friend, Déagol. It was Déagol who first discovered the One Ring on the river bottom. At first glint of its gold, Sméagol was tormented by the desire to seize and possess the One Ring. With virtually no thought to consequences, Sméagol murdered his kinsman and friend, then seized the One Ring.

Déagol's name literally meant "secret". This was doubly appropriate, as the cursed Sméagol always insisted on his ownership of the Ring. His darkest secret was that he had acquired the Ring through murder and theft. Sméagol's conflict is quite similar to the legendary alchemist Faust, who gained wisdom and wealth by making a pact with the Devil.

In Goethe's variation of his life, Faust chooses to betray his conscience and his friend: "Two souls, alas, are in my breast, and one is striving to foresake his brother." On a less conscious level, Sméagol's guilt and fear overwhelm him. Frightened that someone might discover his "secret", Sméagol takes his "Precious" treasure and exiles himself from all his kin. He hides himself away, "burrowing and worming in" beneath the roots of the Misty Mountains.

So, in "hobgoblin", we have a word that embodies the struggle between the forces of the good Hobbit and evil Goblin. There seems no doubt that in Sméagol-Gollum we have a prime example of a hobgoblin, wherein the Goblin entirely overwhelmed the Hobbit. If Bilbo Baggins were the original Hobbit, then, in this ghoulish mockery of Hobbit life, Sméagol-Gollum was the original anti-Hobbit.

Dr Jekyll and Mr Gollum

In Gollum, we have a classic case of split personality, as first portrayed in Robert Louis Stevenson's *Dr Jekyll and Mr Hyde* or in Charles Dickens's *Mystery of Edwin Drood*. In Gollum's case, it is not Jekyll and Hyde, but Sméagol (the Hob) and Gollum (the Goblin). When the Sméagol was in control, he had pale eyes and referred to himself as "I". Gollum, however, was a green-eyed creature who called himself "we" because the Gollum and the Ring spoke as one. Just as in Stevenson's tale, it is this evil personality that overwhelms the good.

Whatever Gollum's obvious defects, one had to admire his ability to survive. Even taking into account the legendary renown of Hobbits for stubbornness,

Sméagol-Gollum was remarkably enduring. In many other respects, Sméagol-Gollum retained other aspects of his Hobbit nature that likely saved him many times from his foes. Typically, when Gollum held the One Ring, he never used its power to any great extent or for any great purpose. As a Hobbit, he was almost totally lacking in any ambition or desire for power. Gollum's desire seemed limited to that of a miser with his gold. Alone in the darkness with his "Precious", this was as close to contentment as the tortured soul of Gollum ever came. Yet Gollum's insistence on his ownership of the One Ring was a delusion. Gollum no more possessed the One Ring than an addict possesses a drug. The Ring was his addiction, not his possession. The Ring, in fact, possessed Gollum. If this were paradise, one must wonder what damnation held in store for him. Far better and stranger was Sméagol-Gollum's true fate. For in Gollum's last evil act of betrayal, Sméagol-Gollum unintentionally martyred himself and brought about the salvation of all the Free People of Middle-earth.

In Gollum's final desperate struggle with Frodo on the edge of Mount Doom, the Hob and the Goblin are locked in a wrestlers' shadow play that has been repeated time and again by the champions of civilizations in historic ages: Gilgamesh of

Mesopotamia, Indra of India, and Heracles of Greece. Each combatant strives to overcome giants and monsters of other nations and bring peace to the world.

In the struggle of the Hobbit and the Gollum, we have a midget wrestling version of the Anglo-Saxon's Beowulf locked in mortal combat with the monster Grendel. In Tolkien's Middle-earth, the fate of the world is determined by the least of its champions, and the struggle for the fate of the World is more a personal struggle over the fate of one's soul. Even so, everything seems to have gone wrong. The Hobbit is doubly defeated – morally by the power of the Ring and physically by the power of Gollum. As the power of Beowulf's superhuman grip allows the hero to tear Grendel's arm from his shoulder socket, so the power of Gollum's supernatural grip (and his Orkish fangs) allows the anti-hero to sever the Hobbit's finger and claim the One Ring that encircles it. Yet upon Middle-earth, the victory of evil often leads to its own defeat. So it proved with Gollum's victory as he falls into the volcano. He ends up as a reluctant martyr whose evil intent resulted in the greatest good.

Left Readers cannot fail to see Gollum's fall into the fires of Mount Doom as symbolic of the Fall of Man, when corrupted by evil and greed for power.

Northmen of Rhovanion

Germania – empire of the north

Of the Northmen of Rhovanion, Tolkien wrote: "Men in those parts remain more or less uncorrupted if ignorant. The better and nobler sort of Men are in fact the kin of those that had departed to Númenor, but remain in a simple 'Homeric' state of patriarchal and tribal life." The Northmen were in truth very like the continental ancestors of that "Homeric" state of patriarchal and tribal life that was celebrated in early Anglo-Saxon epic poetry. The Northmen of Wilderland were the heroic forebears of Beowulf who made their home for millennia in the trackless forests, mountains, and river vales.

Rhovanion was intended to resemble what the ancient Romans called Germania: the Great Northern Forest of Europe. Tolkien gives us a wild eastern frontier comparable to the Russian steppes. And just as the Roman Empire faced wave after wave of the Hun, Tartar, and Mongol invaders, so the Northmen faced the recurring hostile attacks of the Easterlings.

Although historians write of this time as the decline and fall of Rome, others saw a vital and active people flooding into the empire. From their perspective, they were a fluid but reasonably uniform culture which rapidly grafted itself onto the weakened but revered Empire of Rome. No invading nation wished to bring about the empire's fall. Indeed, even its most barbaric conquerers believed that the Roman Empire would never be destroyed. In one form or another, it had existed for more than 1000 years. The Northmen saw simply another evolution, as an even greater and revitalized form of a German-Roman Empire.

Europe in the seventh and eighth centuries was a sparsely populated continent. But this does not mean that people lived alone. Groups of Germanic families usually settled together in villages and groups of villages with their fields surrounded by forest, scrub or marshland. These settlements were mostly self-contained, small oases of cultivated land in a vast uncultivated continent. The forests provided building and heating materials, and game for food and sport. But German paganism centered on the worship of trees, and thus there was a taboo on the destruction of forests.

In the Northmen of Rhovanion we see something of the German tribes at their earliest stages of migration. They were a noble people who did not greatly diminish the forest or plough up the plains – rural people with only a few large, substantial towns and villages. They dwelt in the forests, hills, and vales of Rhovanion. Among them were those known as the Beornings and Woodmen of Mirkwood, and the Bardings, or Men of Dale. To the south on the horse plains of Rohan were the Rohirrim, "the Masters of Horses", who were akin to the historic Goths, "horse folk".

We should also look to the history of the Frankish kingdoms in the eighth century to discover what inspired Tolkien's Northmen. None of the other barbarian successor states to the Roman Empire had been even remotely in a position to threaten them seriously, and the Byzantines were much too far away to attempt the reconquest of Gaul as they had attempted the reconquest of Italy. But in the early eighth century the geopolitical situation changed. The Saracens, ie the Arabs and the North African Muslims had conquered Visigothic Spain and soon they crossed the Pyrenees into Gaul. The defeat of these invaders in 732 enormously enhanced the prestige of the Carolingians, the dynasty that would give rise to Charlemagne.

In resonance with this period of European history, at the time of War of the Ring, Tolkien has his Northmen under threat from outside invaders and drawn into alliances with the other free peoples of Middle-earth in mutual defence. The ensuing conflict also gives rise to a great leader and king, Aragorn.

Tolkien's Middle-earth is a world in which the archetypes of our own history were geographically laid out and written about as if seen through the eyes of the ancient English. In a sense, it is an infusion of both England writ large and the whole of Europe in the Golden Age of the Goths – the vast loose alliance of the ancient Germanic peoples.

Beornings – bears and berserkers

Northmen were first encountered by Bilbo Baggins in *The Hobbit*, in the singular form of the eponymous Beorn, chieftain of the Beornings. Beorn was a huge, black-bearded man garbed in a coarse wool tunic and armed with a woodsman's axe. Although vengeful in his slaughter of Orcs and Wargs, Beorn ate no meat and killed no creatures of the forest. Despite his imposing size, deer would approach him and allow him to stroke them without fear.

For the most part, the Beornings of West Mirkwood and their kinsmen, the Woodmen of East Mirkwood, were in temperament and nature very like Beorn. Often brutal and ruthless with foes, in the company of friends and allies, they were extremely kind-hearted and gentle. In appearance, as well as nobility of spirit, the Beornings and Woodlanders were akin to their chieftain, except in stature and rank.

Beorn appears to be something approaching a Middle-earth twin brother of Beowulf, the epic hero of the Anglo-Saxons. With his pride in his strength, his code of honour, his terrible wrath, his hospitality, and even the structure of the small-scale variation of the Great Hall of Hrothgar in *Beowulf* – in all things but the difference of scale between epic and fairy-tale realms – Beorn is Beowulf.

In fact, Tolkien, by way of a philological manipulation, gives his character a name which sounds and looks different, but in the end is really the same animal. "Beorn" is a keeper of bees and a lover of honey. His name means "man" in Old English; however, in its Norse form, it means "bear". Meanwhile, if we look at the Old English name "Beowulf", we discover it literally and strangely means "bee-wolf".

What is a bee-wolf? This is typical of the sort of riddle-name the ancient Anglo-Saxons liked to construct. "What 'wolf' hunts bees – and steals their honey?" The answer is obvious enough: "bee-wolf" means "bear". Beowulf and Beorn both mean "bear". One might say that Beowulf and Beorn are the same men with different names, or, in their symbolic guise as the bee-wolf and the bear, they are the same animal in different skins.

The serious point to this word play was that, through Beorn, Tolkien reveals his own theory of Beowulf's origin, in the rituals of the ancient bear cults of the Teutonic peoples. Among the most ancient of all Eurasian cults, bear cults were the inspiration for the terrifying and bizarre displays of "holy battle rage". This rage was famously exhibited by those Teutonic warriors who became known as "Berserkers". These were Odin's warriors who charged in battle – often wearing only animal skins. As Odin's holy warriors, they sometimes went into battle unarmed and in such a rage that they tore the enemy limb from limb with their bare hands and teeth. They were the holy warriors of Odin, lord of battles. At their moment of death, Odin would send the Valkyries, his winged battle maidens. The Valkyries would carry the heroes over the Rainbow Bridge to Valhalla, the Great Hall of the Slain. This was the heaven of heroes, where they feasted and drank until they were called upon for the Last Battle of the End of Time at the World's End.

In *The Hobbit*, Tolkien gives us the fairy-tale version of the character of the cultural hero Beorn, as the founder of the Beornings (the "man-bear" people). The tale of Beorn was also written in support of Tolkien's belief in the origin of Beowulf as a similar man-bear "skin-changer" and the bear-cult hero of the Berserkers (ie "bear-sark", or "bear-shirts"). Although the historical Berserkers felt possessed by the ferocious spirit of the enraged bear, these states were only rituals attempting to imitate the core miracle of the cult: the incarnate transformation of man to bear. This is exactly what Tolkien provides within the fairy story of his Beorn–Beowulf hero in his miraculous transformation in the Battle of Five Armies before the Dragon Gate of the Lonely Mountain.

Once again, Tolkien used a name as an oracle: "Beorn" can mean either "bear" or "man". Soon enough, Beorn is revealed as a "skin-changer". This is the power of transformation: man to beast, beast to man. This is the blood inheritance of Beorn from Beren the Edain hero and Sigmund the Volsung hero as fellow skin-

changers and forest-dwelling vegetarians. The Scandinavian *Saga of King Hrolk Kraki* also features a character called Bjorn, the "man-bear". He meets a tragic end; whilst in the form of a bear he is hunted and killed by humans. Perhaps this could explain the characterization of Tolkien's Beorn, his distrust of men and his wary nature. In *Kraki*, Bjorn's son, Bodvar Bjarki inherits some of his father's supernatural qualities. He appears at King Hrolf's final battle in the form of a huge bear, invulnerable to weapons. The highly public battlefield transformation of Beorn the warrior into the "Were-Bear" was an event that turned the tide of the Battle of the Five Armies. It also dramatically provided the followers of the bear cult with its core miracle upon which the rituals and rites of passage for the Berserker warriors might be founded.

Black arrow of the dragonslayer

Another branch of these Northmen was the merchants of Esgaroth, who lived in the city of Dale and the Lake Town of Esgaroth. When the fire-dragon Smaug the Golden descends he is slain by a single arrow shot by another hero of Middle-earth.

It may have been Apollo who provided the inspiration for the slaying of Smaug the Golden. All other dragonslayers in myth have killed their monsters with

Above The hospitality offered by Beorn to Thorin and Company in *The Hobbit* within his wooden hall is a smaller-scale imitation of that archetype of all mead halls, Valhalla, to which the fallen warriors of Odin are carried by the Valkyries, winged battle-maidens.

ritualistic ancestral swords. For some reason, only Apollo the Archer and Bard the Bowman are capable of slaying their dragons with arrows.

In ancient Greece, dragons guarded treasures and wells or caves of a sacred or prophetic nature. The most famous dragon of that time was one known as the Python of Delphi, who made his lair in the mountain pass and sacred oracle of Delphi. The slayer of Python was Apollo the sun god, who was also the god of music, knowledge, medicine, youth, and poetry. Apollo was also "lord of archers" with his silver bow and deadly arrows, and he slew the dragon.

There is a critical moment in the dragonslaying episode of *The Hobbit*, that is a distant curious echo of another famous incident in Greek myth and literature involving Apollo and a mortal archer. Just at the moment that the Dragon's destruction of the town seems certain, and Bard draws his last black arrow, a little bird whispers in the ear of the Bowman. The bird reveals the secret of Smaug's "Achilles heel": the one fatal spot where an arrow might pierce the Dragon's otherwise impenetrable body. In the midst of the Trojan War, when the terrifying rage of Achilles' destruction of the city seems certain, and Paris draws back his last arrow, Apollo whispers in the ear of the Trojan. The god reveals the secret of Achilles heel: the one fatal spot where an arrow might pierce the hero's otherwise impenetrable body. Both heroes take the advice, both cities are saved, and Smaug the Golden and Achilles are slain.

The bow and arrow are known from early Neolithic times. Flint arrow-heads are among the most common archaeological discoveries from that era. It can safely be assumed that the prestige of the bowman goes a very long way back in human history. So, too, perhaps, goes the drama of the last shot, when the enemy is still unslain and only one arrow remains. This is the situation which JRR Tolkien exploits with great dramatic effect in the death of Smaug. The performer of the deed is no ordinary man. He is Bard, heir to the kings of Dale. A terse, grim individual, it is he who takes command as the Dragon circles the vulnerable wooden houses of Lake Town. And it is his last arrow that finds the dragon's vulnerable spot and kills it. In a suspenseful and dramatic tale, this is exactly how it should be; the Dragon's death too soon makes everything easy, and the telling tedious. And, in a well-crafted story, there is more to come. By his deed, Bard takes revenge for the destruction of his home city, and establishes his right to reclaim its kingship. He is in the classic mould of a hero, the saviour of the remnant of his people and the promise of regeneration to come. The circle is fully turned; satisfaction is complete. Bard's taciturn quality seems to be inherent in famous archers; it is certainly shared with another legendary bowman. Wilhelm Tell had two arrows in his quiver when the Tyrant Gessler forced him to shoot the apple off his young son's head. When asked afterwards by the Austrian what the second one was needed for, Tell replied, "For you, had I missed."

The Horsemen of Rohan

Goths and Mercians

The Horsemen of Rohan were the supreme cavalrymen of Middle-earth. Like the historic Goth cavalrymen on the plains east and north of the Western and Eastern Roman Empires, the Riders of Rohan, or Rohirrim, commanded the plain of Rohan and the Mark, and defended the passes into the Kingdoms of Arnor and Gondor. Both the Goths and the Rohirrim were constantly prepared for battle and similar in appearance and temperament. In fact, the charge of the Rohirrim in the Battle of the Pelennor Fields towards the end of the War of the Ring is based on historic Roman account of Goth and Lombard cavalries.

Tolkien was fascinated with the Goths, ever since as a student he had stumbled on a book of Gothic grammar. In Gothic, Tolkien saw the first recorded language of the Germanic people and the first recorded language spoken by the progenitors of the English people. Tolkien believed that through his study of the language, and the surviving fragments of Gothic texts, he would gain new insights into this elusive people. He found a considerable amount to interest him in the fifth-century court of the first Gothic Emperor Theodoric the Great, who was the inspiration for many epic tales and romances. Theodoric was a kind of Germanic Hercules, known as Wolfdietrich, and later Dietrich von Berne.

Although the Riders of Rohan have much historically in common with the Goths, in their characterization (except for the overwhelming significance of the horse in their culture) they are almost entirely akin to the ancient Anglo-Saxons. Essentially, in the Rohirrim we have Beowulf's people, plus horses.

When Gandalf rode toward Rohan's royal city of Edoras, Tolkien describes the distant sight of the gold roof of the Golden Hall of Meduseld glinting in the sunlight. The name "Meduseld" in fact, is ancient Anglo-Saxon for "mead hall". The description of the hall is almost identical to that of Herot, the Golden Hall of King Hrothgar in *Beowulf*. As Beowulf approaches the kingdom of Hrothgar, the poet catches sight of Herot's roof gables covered with hammered gold that glistens and glints in the light of the sun. Both of these great halls have even greater divine models. Meduseld has its divine model in Valinor in the Great Hall of Oromë the Horseman, and Herot's Hall has the Great Hall of Valhalla as its divine model. This was the "Hall of Slain Heroes", roofed with golden shields. It was the mead hall and heaven of fallen warriors, created for them in Asgard by Odin.

The Rohirrim were also named the "Riders of the Mark". The term "mark", or "march", meant a "borderland" and referred to land occupied by an independent

Right While many peoples throughout history have used cavalry as part of their armed forces, the Riders of Rohan bear closest comparison to the cavalrymen of the Goths and their role in the defence of the Roman empire.

Right Meduseld in the land of Rohan bears a close resemblance to Herot, the Golden Hall of King Hrothgar in the Anglo-Saxon poem *Beowulf*.

ally to serve as a buffer between two hostile nations. Famously, the Franks of Charlemagne set up the Dane Mark as a buffer between themselves and the pagan nations of Scandinavia. In Britain, the Romans established the Welsh Marches, which the Anglo-Saxons called the "Mark" or "Mearc". This became the kingdom of Mercia, a name by which the region is sometimes still known today. For a time, it became the most powerful kingdom in Britain and, along with Northumbria and Wessex, produced the first true Anglo-Saxon kings of England. This was the heartland of England and Tolkien's own homeland.

In the same period that Tolkien began writing *The Lord of the Rings*, Tolkien took his family to visit White Horse Hill. It was less than 32km (20 miles) from his home in Oxford. This is the site of the famous image of the gigantic White Horse cut into the chalk beneath the green turf and topsoil on the hill. There is no doubt that this is the White Horse which gave JRR Tolkien the image of a white horse on a green field which marked the banners for the Rohirrim.

Saviours of Rome and Gondor

The Horsemen of Rohan and the Kingdoms of Gondor and Arnor have a history comparable to that of the Goths and the Empire of Rome. In the fifth century AD, the Goths made their most dramatic rescue of the Roman Empire. It was one of the most decisive battles in Western history, and the invader was the most formidable the Romans had ever faced – Attila the Hun. It was a pivotal moment: had the Huns been victorious that day, it is certain that the Asiatic invasion would have resulted in the subjugation of all Europe. In the second millennium of the Third Age both Kingdoms of the Dúnedain were on the point of being overrun by barbarian invaders known as the Easterlings. The Rohirrim cavalry came at the critical moment to the Field of Celebrant, crushed and destroyed the Easterling forces, and drove them back to their own lands.

After the retreat of the invading Huns, the Goths became the main inheritors of lands devastated by the barbarians of the Western Roman Empire. It was now clear that these Goth tribesmen were no longer seen as barbarians, but were a vital part of the empire. In both the Western and Eastern Roman Empires, the Goths were given lands of their own as reward for their military services. Meanwhile, as reward for their salvation that day, Gondor gave the Riders the land called Rohan, meaning "Land of the Horselords", in their honour. And in these lands, the Rohirrim were able to live as free men under their own kings and laws, but always in alliance with Gondor.

The shield-maiden, Éowyn of Rohan, who kills the Witch-king in battle, belongs to an ancient tradition within this world of epic romance and saga. She is the idealized model for the historic figures in the Norse *Volsunga Saga* and the German *Nibelungenlied*, and the twin characters of Brynhild and Brunhild, from both. In *The Volsunga Saga* Brynhild was a Valkyrie, a beautiful battle maiden who defied Odin and was subsequently pierced with a sleep-thorn and imprisoned in a ring of fire. Like Sleeping Beauty she is awakened from sleep, by Sigurd the Dragonslayer, with whom she falls in love. In the *Nibelungenlied*, Brunhild (which means 'armoured warrior maid') is the warrior-queen of Iceland, who falls for the Sigurd equivalent, Siefried. Both Brynhild and Brunhild are based on the historic and notorious Visigoth Queen Brunhilda.

Just as there are elements of Brynhild/Brunhild to be found in Éowyn, so there are comparisons to be drawn between Sigurd/Siegfried and Aragorn. Likewise,

Above The Mearas were the magical horses ridden by the Rohirrim. Two in particular feature prominently in *The Lord of the Rings*; Snowmane, who lost his life in the Battle of Pelennor Fields along with his mount, King Théoden, and Shadowfax, the steed of Gandalf the White.

it is Bryhild/Brunhild's hopeless love for Sigurd/Siegfried that Tolkien draws on for Éowyn's own unrequited feelings for Aragorn. Siegfried, for example, is betrothed to another queen, Kriemheld, in the same way that Aragorn is to Arwen of Rivendell. And as the Warrior Queen Brunhild is transformed by marriage into the gentle and subservient wife of Gunnar, so too is Éowyn, through her wedding to Faramir.

Troy on the Rhine

The heroic age for all the nations of Northern Europe was the chaotic fifth, sixth and seventh centuries AD, known as the Dark Ages, the time after the collapse of Rome and before the rise of the Holy Roman Empire. The historical chieftains of those times became the subjects of oral traditions that elevated them to mythic status. It was a heroic age equivalent to the Ancient Greeks chaotic eleventh, tenth, and ninth centuries BC, that generated Homer's epic masterpieces *The Iliad* and *The Odyssey*.

The historic destruction of Troy was the catastrophic event that inspired the literary masterpieces of the Greek people. In Northern Europe there was an equivalent catastrophe, the annihilation of the Burgundians in 436 AD by a contingent of Huns under the leadership of Attila, acting as mercenary agents for the

Right In *The Volsunga Saga*, the hero Sigurd, mounted on his horse Grani, discovers the sleeping warrior-maiden Brynhild on a bier. After succumbing to the Black Breath of the Witch-king at the Battle of Pelennor Fields, Éowyn too falls into a death-like sleep, but is eventually awakened when Aragorn gives her the healing herb athelas (kingsfoil).

Roman Empire. The memory of the catastrophic end of the entire warrior elite and the extermination of a once-powerful people was recalled vividly by the neighbouring Franks. The story of the Burgundians on the Rhine was told and retold by the Visigoths, Saxons, Ostrogoths, Lombards, Austrians, and Norsemen.

In just over a millennium the Burgundian tragedy had become the most influential catastrophe in European literature since the Fall of Troy. Those who doubt this might consider just a small part of the literature inspired by the event. It was the catalyst for *The Volsunga Saga*, the national epic of Norway and Iceland. It provided the basis for the *Nibelungenlied* the national epic romance of Germany and Austria. It also provided the inspiration for Wagner's opera, *The Ring of the Nibelung*.

Curiously, all three of these works: the saga, the epic romance and the opera have a single common motif of the ring quests. All three, along with the original historic incident, have had a profound influence on the *The Lord of the Rings*.

Men of Gondor

Ancient Rome and Gondor

If one looks to the history of Rome, it is not difficult to recognize the chronicles of this ancient imperial power in the epic of Middle-earth; there are many aspects of Rome's history comparable to the ancient history of Gondor.

According to Virgil, the progenitor of the Romans was Prince Aeneas, the son of a mortal nobleman and the immortal goddess Venus. Aeneas survived the destruction of the royal city of Troy, then sailed for many years lost in the paths of many enchanted isles. With the help of the goddess Venus, Aeneas travelled to the Isle of the Blessed, then returned to guide his people into the western sea and their promised land of Italy. Generations later, the descendants of Aeneas – two brothers – founded Rome: a city and civilization that was destined to create an empire that would rule the world.

According to Tolkien, the progenitor of the Dúnedain was Prince Eärendil, the child of an Edain mortal nobleman and an immortal Elven princess. Eärendil survived the destruction of the royal city of Gondolin, then sailed for many years lost in the paths through the Enchanted Isles. With the help of the Princess Elwing, Eärendil travels to the Land of the Blessed, then returns to guide his people into the western sea and settle them in this new promised land of Númenor (which Tolkien based on the myth of Atlantis). Generations later, the descendants of Eärendil – once again two brothers – founded Gondor: a city and civilization that was destined to create an empire that would rule Middle-earth.

Perhaps the oddest element connecting the two heroes is the immortal aspects of both men. Strangely enough, the mother of Prince Aeneas is the goddess Venus, while Eärendil the Mariner becomes an immortal custodian of the light source that *is* Venus. This is not the goddess, of course, but rather the planet Venus, which is also the morning and evening star whose light Eärendil bears aloft each night as he sails across the sky.

Curiously, the involvement of brothers in the founding of nations proves doubly significant on Middle-earth. In the case of Rome, the twin brothers – famously raised by wolves – are Romulus and Remus. In Númenor (Atlantis), the twin brothers are Elros and Elrond, the Half-elven sons of Eärendil and Elwing. In both cases, however, only one of each, Romulus and Elros, respectively, establishes a dynastic line of kings. By contrast, Gondor is founded by two brothers (but not twins), Isildur and Anárion, who become joint rulers and both independently establish dynastic lines of kings.

THE WAR OF THE RING III

As we have already seen, the Easterling barbarian hordes (in service of the evil eye of Sauron the Necromancer) that menaced the Dúnedain empire's eastern borders find an exact parallel in accounts of the waves of Hunnish and Teutonic barbarians hordes (in service of the one-eyed Odin the Necromancer) that menaced the Roman Empire's borders.

Similarly, Gondor's great rivals to the south were the Black Númenórean Lords of Umbar. "Umbar" means "fate", and it truly seemed that Gondor and Umbar were locked in a fatal conflict. Umbar's mighty war fleets were the terror of the seas, while the city's powerful mercenary armies, which were supported by war elephants and Saracen-like cavalries, were a terror on land. This is comparable to the earlier history of Rome, whose great rivals to the south had been the lords of Carthage, whose mighty war fleets were the terror of the seas, and whose powerful mercenary armies were supported by war elephants and Saracen cavalries.

Theseus and Aragorn

A comparison between Gondor and Athens is not often made, but a resemblance does exist, most evidently in the legend of the hero Theseus who became king of Athens. To begin with, the Citadel of Gondor and the Acropolis of Athens have identical traditions of the sacred Fountain and Tree (for the ancient Greeks, it was an olive tree; in Gondor, it was the White Tree of the Elves). Furthermore, the Citadel of Gondor is similar in basic structure to the Acropolis, including the ship-prow ridge. From the heights of the Acropolis, the Athenians could look down the 50km (30 miles) of the "Long Walls" which linked Athens to its ports on the Aegean Sea, just as Gondor's citizens looked down on the Great Wall Circle that linked the city to her ports on the River Anduin.

In *The Lord of the Rings*, during the siege of Gondor, there is one episode that almost exactly mirrors the climax of the famous Greek myth of Theseus. In the Greek tale, the hero is revealed as the true heir to the throne of Athens. His father welcomes him back (despite fatal prophecies of regicide). When Theseus discovers that Athens must pay an annual tribute of seven youths and seven maidens as sacrificial victims to the Minoans, however, he decides to end this bloody payment. Theseus sets out in a black-sailed tribute ship to Crete where, along with other Athenians, he is to be sacrificed to the monstrous Minotaur in the palace of King Minos. Upon departure, however, Theseus promises his father, the king of Athens that, if he slays the Minotaur and releases his people from bondage, he will change the sails to white for his return voyage as a signal of victory.

In the flush of his triumph, however, Theseus forgets his promise. Tragically, his father, the old king, sees the tribute ship returning with its great black sail still

Left The knights of Gondor remained proud and fearless, despite their dwindling numbers and the gradual decline of their kingdom prior to the War of the Ring.

set. Believing his son to be dead, and his nation still enslaved, the old king throws himself from the high lookout prow of the Acropolis onto the rocks far below.

In *The Lord of the Rings*, we have Denethor, the Ruling Steward of Gondor, who sees a mighty fleet of the black-sailed ships of the Corsairs of Umbar sailing up the Anduin River at a critical moment in the Battle of the Pelennor Fields, which takes place towards the climax of the War of the Ring. By this time, the Great Gate of Gondor has been shattered by the Witch-king, Denethor's only surviving son appears to be dying of a poison wound, and all his forces upon the battlefield are moments away from being overwhelmed and slaughtered. The Steward is correct in assuming that the enemy reinforcements in the black-sailed ships would doom his warriors once and for all, and make the defence of Gondor impossible. Denethor's will is now broken. He gives way to the self-indulgence of despair. (A true leader of Men such as Aragorn cannot give way to such pride. First and last, he must act and serve his subjects.) Mad with despair, Denethor reads the signs wrongly and, upon seeing the Black Sails of the Ships of Umbar, commits suicide; however, like Theseus's father, the Steward of Gondor was tragically mistaken.

Like Theseus, too, Aragorn had undergone a terrible ordeal by passing through an underground labyrinth known as the Paths of the Dead, after the Battle of Helm's Deep. When Aragorn emerged, it was as the King of the Dead Men of Dunharrow, and he commanded this terrifying army of the undead warriors against the Corsairs of Umbar. Caught unprepared in the port of Pelargir, the Corsairs fled in terror at this Shadow Host. The black-sailed ships of the Corsairs were seized by Aragorn. They were then used to gather and carry fighting men fresh into the Battle of the Pelennor Fields. It was the decisive stroke of the battle, and the enemy was trapped between "hammer and anvil", and so crushed.

Just as Athens is freed from the threat of the tyrant and Theseus succeeds his father as king, so Gondor is freed from the threat of the Witch-king, and Aragorn is restored as the true king of the Reunited Kingdom of Gondor and Arnor.

From Byzantium to Egypt

From another perspective, it is possible to compare the Western Empire of Rome with the Northern Kingdom of Arnor. We discover Arnor's division into Arthedain, Rhudaur, and Cardolan, which is rather prophetic of the fate of Western Roman Empire's division into its three spheres of influence: Italy, Germany, and France. In the efforts of Aragorn II in the War of the Ring, we have a warrior king who manages to re-establish the ancient lands of his ancestors in a single reunited Kingdom. Aragorn II is presented with the double crown of the kingdoms of Arnor and Gondor. In so doing, Aragorn created the precedent (or so

Left While obviously mirroring the pirate ships of both the Carthaginian and Ottoman empires, the Black Ships of Umbar in the War of the Ring most closely correspond to the vessel sailed by Theseus in the ancient Greek legend of the Minotaur.

Tolkien would have us believe) for the historic warlord Charlemagne's reconquest and re-establishment of the Roman Empire. Consequently, on New Year's Day of 800 AD, Charlemagne was crowned the first "Emperor of the Romans".

Certainly, we could also compare the early Dúnedain kingdom with the ancient Roman Empire. Observing the division of the historic Western Roman Empire and the Eastern Byzantine Empire, it is reasonably easy to match them up with Gondor and Arnor. The disastrous military and social history of the North Kingdom of Arnor and its subsequent collapse was comparable to the true history of the Western Roman Empire. They differ mostly because the fall of the historic Empire in the West was more rapid, and far more brutal.

Gondor's three great cities were located on either side and astride the Great River Anduin as it passes through the only gap through two mountain ranges (the White and Shadowy Mountain ranges). All travel, whether by river, boat, cart,

horseback, or foot, had to be made through that narrow gap to reach any of the lands to the west and south of Gondor. Compare Gondor to the historic city of Constantinople (one part in Europe and the other in Asia) and imagine the Black Land of Mordor as the Black Sea, then strategically Gondor is also perfectly positioned to control trade between east and west. Constantinople controlled the only waterway to the Mediterranean Sea with one port on the Black Sea and the other on the Hellespont. So, too, Gondor controlled the bottleneck, and her cities straddled the Anduin River and the roadways to the sea.

Tolkien himself further remarked on the character of the Men of Gondor: "The Númenóreans of Gondor were proud, peculiar, and archaic, and I think are best pictured in (say) Egyptian terms. In many ways they resemble 'Egyptians' – the love of, and power to construct, the gigantic and massive. And their great interest in ancestry and in tombs. (But not of course in 'theology': in which respect they were Hebraic and even more puritan…) I think the crown of Gondor (the South Kingdom) was very tall, like that of Egypt, but with wings attached, not set straight back but at an angle. The North Kingdom had only a diadem – Cf. the difference between the North and South kingdoms of Egypt."

Gondor and the White Tower

"A city could never be happy otherwise than by imitating the divine pattern," Plato wrote in *The Republic*. In Plato's view, God is the maker of patterns behind the material world of illusions, and the octave is a primary form in the pattern of music as it relates tone to number and both to geometry.

In the creation of the city and fortress of Minas Tirith on seven levels with seven walls and seven gates in duplication of the tones of an octave (with the eighth note being twice the span of the first), Tolkien is consistent with traditions dating back at least 5000 years to ancient Sumeria. There the goddess Ianna descends through the seven walls and seven gates of hell. Also, the biblical paradise of Eden is surrounded by seven walls and has seven gates. Islam, however, is not content with one heaven. It has an intentional musical structure of seven heavens in rising levels of grandeur, until the seventh transcendental level is reached.

In Renaissance literature, there were many Utopias and Dystopias constructed on the octave. In Dante's conception of Heaven and Hell, the structure of both reflect this pattern. Tommaso Campanella (1568–1639) is particularly memorable for his structuring of seven levels in imitation of the Music of the Spheres in his *City of the Sun*. It seems likely that Tolkien had the *City of the Sun* at the back of his mind, as Gondor, city of the White Tower, was originally called Minas Anor, or "Tower of the Sun".

To compensate for the disaster that had struck his people's legendary forebears, Plato created an idealized Athens. Like Minas Tirith, this ideal Athens was structured on the geometric forming of octave circles and an ideal system of "equal temperament" that allows for all adjustments, celestial and temporal. Likewise, in order to make up for the disaster that befell the kingdom of Númenor, it seems that Tolkien is giving his readers Gondor to see if the Dúnedain have learned from the mistakes of their once proud ancestors.

Left In an archetypal clash of good and evil, white and dark power, Gandalf the White Wizard challenges and overwhelms the Lieutenant of Barad-dûr at the Gates of Mordor. Victory in the War of the Ring restores harmony to the lands of Middle-earth.

The Reunited Kingdom of the Dúnedain

Future kings – Aragorn, Arthur, and Sigurd

English-language readers of *The Lord of the Rings* frequently register a connection between the legendary King Arthur and Aragorn. What is not often apparent, however, is that twelfth- to fourteenth-century Arthurian romances are often based on fifth-century Early German-Gothic oral epics – epics that now only survive in the myths of their Norse and Icelandic descendants. Tolkien was far more interested in these early Germanic elements of the tale linking Aragorn with Sigurd the Volsung, the archetypal hero of the Teutonic Ring Legend.

Although all three heroic warrior kings are clearly similar, the context for all three – in pagan saga, medieval romance, and modern fantasy – is very different. The creation of a medieval King Arthur and the court of Camelot, with its Christian moral principles, naturally resulted in some reshaping of many of the fiercer aspects of the early pagan tradition. Sigurd the Volsung is a wild warrior who would have been out of place at Arthur's polite, courtly round table. Curiously, although Tolkien's Aragorn is indeed a pagan hero, he is often even more upright and moral than the medieval Christian King Arthur.

Despite these differences of context, however, the comparison of Arthur, Sigurd, and Aragorn demonstrates the power of archetypes, especially in dictating aspects of character in the heroes of legend and myth. If we look at the lives of each of these three, we see certain patterns that are identical: Arthur, Sigurd, and Aragorn are all orphaned sons and rightful heirs to kings slain in battle; all are deprived of their inherited kingdoms and are in danger of assassination; all are the last of their dynasty, their noble lineage ending if they are slain; all are raised secretly in foster homes under the protection of a foreign noble who is a distant relative – Arthur is raised in the castle of Sir Ector, Sigurd in the hall of King Hjalprek, and Aragorn in Rivendell in the house of Elrond.

During their fostering – in childhood and as youths – all three heroes achieve feats of strength and skill that mark them for future greatness. They all fall in love with beautiful maidens, but must overcome several seemingly impossible obstacles before they can marry: Arthur to Guinevere, Sigurd to Brynhild, Aragorn to Arwen. However, by overcoming these obstacles they win both love and their kingdoms.

There is much in Aragorn that is resonant, not just with Arthur and Sigurd, but many heroes of other nations. In Aragorn, we have essentially the ideal warrior-

king of every age. He is the central figure in a dynastic history that begins over 6000 years back in the annals of Middle-earth's history. Strider is Aragorn II, Chieftain of the North Kingdom. He is chosen as the redeeming hero, and liberator of Middle-earth. In the life of Aragorn, JRR Tolkien creates his ideal Myth-Time hero and, in so doing, gives expression and definition to what the cultural anthropologist, Joseph Campbell, has called the "Hero-With-A-Thousand-Faces". Joseph Campbell presented the theory that all mythologies can be understood as parts of one universal myth cycle, which he calls the "Monomyth".

The Monomyth is a single great ring of tales marking out each stage in the hero's life: from birth to death; then on again, through resurrection to rebirth. Ultimately all heroes are one hero; and all myths are one myth. The eternal circle or ring is like a serpent swallowing its own tail/tale. Of course, Tolkien created Aragorn long before Campbell developed his theories, but Tolkien had theories of his own. The reason for Aragorn's resemblance to Campbell's universal hero is that both authors view the mythic dimension as a timeless sacred realm of numerous ideal entities and archetypes. This is also why – Tolkien suggests – the lives of many of the heroes of Middle-earth are often comparable to heroes of the Primary World, and why the heroes of myths and fairy tales have an imperfect resemblance to the ideal heroes of Middle-earth's Myth Time. This is especially true of Aragorn. Gifted with

Above In Arthurian legend, it is Arthur who unites the numerous British kings who are represented by the Knights of the Round Table. Similarly, it is Aragorn who reunites the fragmented lands of the Dúnedain people under his kingship at the end of the War of the Ring.

a life span three times that of ordinary men, Aragorn is a hero with the time to live through virtually every stage in Campbell's Monomyth.

Dynasties and ancestral swords

The significance of the ancestral sword of the warrior king is naturally critical to all three heroes. King Arthur is famous for the contest of Excalibur, or the Sword in the Stone. This is an act that duplicates the contest in *The Volsunga Saga*, when Sigurd's father Sigmund alone can draw the sword, Balmung, which Odin has driven into Branstock, the living "roof-tree" which is the central pillar in the Great Hall of the Volsungs (symbolically the World Tree of the Norse World and literally the Family Tree of the Volsungs).

Neither Sigurd himself nor Aragorn of the Dúnedain, however, are presented with such contests: they are both given their swords as heirlooms. Their problem is instead that both swords are broken, and neither may use them to reclaim their kingdoms until they are reforged. In Sigurd's case, the sword was broken by Odin in his father Sigmund's last battle, while Aragorn's sword was broken by his ancestor Elendil in his last battle with Sauron. Like the swords of Sigurd and Aragorn, Arthur's sword is supposedly unbreakable; however, through special circumstances, all three are broken. Sigmund's and Aragorn's swords break in battles with supernatural opponents, while King Arthur's sword breaks when he makes an unrighteous attack on Sir Pellinore. It is as if the Christian king's sword is endowed with a moral conscience. Although Arthur's weapon is broken, however, he is not slain, as Sigmund was when his sword broke. Instead, Sir Pellinore is on the point of killing him when Merlin puts Pellinore into a deep swoon. Arthur is saved by the wizard Merlin and undergoes a spiritual resurrection. The penitent and reformed Arthur is reborn. Along similar lines, Sigmund is resurrected in his son Sigurd, just as Elendil is resurrected in his descendant Aragorn.

Once Sigurd reforged his sword Gram, he set out at once to reclaim his heritage. He does this by avenging his father's death and reclaiming his kingdom by conquest, slaying the dragon Fafnir and taking the monster's treasure and ring. Sigurd then goes on to win his beloved Valkyrie princess Brynhild. To some degree, although the ring quest is quite the opposite, Aragorn's life mirrors Sigurd's. Once Aragorn's sword Andúril is reforged, he sets off to reclaim his heritage. He avenges his father's death, reclaims his kingdom by conquest, and, after the destruction of the One Ring, wins his beloved princess, Arwen Evenstar.

The nature of Aragorn's sword owes something to both Arthurian and Volsung traditions. Aragorn's sword was originally named "Narsil", meaning "red and white flame". It was forged by Telchar, the greatest of all the Dwarf-smiths of the

First Age. Narsil is broken by Elendil in a battle with Sauron the Ring Lord and is reforged in Rivendell by the Elves of Celebrimbor, the greatest of all the Elf-smiths of the Second Age. Renamed Andúril, meaning "flame of the west", its blade flickers with a living red flame in sunlight and a white flame in moonlight.

In the Volsung tradition, the sword that Odin drives into Branstock and is then claimed by Sigmund is forged in Alfheim by the hero known to the Saxons as Wayland the Smith. The sword has no formal name until it is reforged for Sigurd by the Dwarf-like Regin the Smith. The sword is then named "Gram", and its blade is distinguished by not only its unbreakable temperament, but also the living light of the blue flames that play along its razor edges.

The tale of King Arthur differs from Sigurd and Aragorn in that he does not have his broken sword reforged. Arthur is instead given a new sword, Excalibur, by the enchantress Viviane, who is also known as the Lady of the Lake. As another boon, Excalibur has a jewelled scabbard that will not allow Arthur to be wounded. The blade of Arthur's Excalibur blade also flickers with a living flame and, like Gram and Andúril, can cleave through iron and stone, yet maintain its razor-sharp edge. Meanwhile, in the Elf Queen Galadriel in the Golden Wood of Lothlórien, we have a comparable figure to Arthur's benefactor, Viviane. Galadriel gives Aragorn a jewelled sheath that makes the sword blade of Andúril unstainable and unbreakable.

The origins of the Holy Roman Empire

As King Arthur was the historic fifth-century national hero of England, celebrated in legend and romance, so the historic ninth-century Emperor Charlemagne was comparably celebrated as the national hero of France; both became powerful national icons. Whenever an old royal dynasty ended in this period of history, the new regime often attempted to legitimize itself by claiming descent from the national hero. By remarkable coincidence, every time a new royal dynasty was established the miraculous discovery of some long lost manuscript or artefact would prove conclusively that the new ruler was the descendant and true heir of the nation's founder.

Charlemagne's heroic status in France was nonsense, as Professor Tolkien might grumpily point out because Charlemagne was no more a Frenchman than King Arthur was an Englishman. Ironically, the historic Arthur's most formidable foes were the earliest Englishmen, particularly the pagan Saxons. The historic Arthur was an early Welsh-speaking British warlord. The Britons had been Christians and Roman citizens for centuries, and their aristocracy spoke Latin, and read Greek. Charlemagne was a German-speaking monarch who also knew Latin and some Greek. He seems to have had no interest in the languages of his subjects west of the Rhine. Charlemagne was the essential German warrior-king, except for one thing,

which made all the difference. This King of the Franks was a Christian sanctified by the Christian Church of Rome, and confirmed by the Pope as the anointed heir to the last Emperor of Rome.

Although the world of Middle-earth was written specifically without religious references, JRR Tolkien often pointed out how many readers saw the connection between Aragorn and King Arthur, but usually missed the connection between Aragorn and Charlemagne. It seemed to Tolkien that in his task of reconstructing the Reunited Kingdom of the Dúnedain from the ruins of the ancient kingdoms of Arnor and Gondor, Aragorn was historically comparable to Charlemagne. Both Aragorn and Charlemagne fought many battles to drive out invaders, and save the inhabitants of their ancient kingdoms. Once their foes were defeated, both Aragorn and Charlemagne, quickly re-established the ancient common laws, set up a common currency, rebuilt the ancient roads and re-established postal systems. Both inspired a golden age of culture, art and literature. Charlemagne became the first Holy Roman Emperor (in all but name, he was actually crowned as "Emperor of the Romans") while Aragorn was renamed Elessar Telcondar, and crowned High King of the Reunited Kingdom of the Dúnedain.

Geographically, Tolkien saw in the Reunited Kingdom an expanse of lands that was far more extensive than King Arthur's lands, and much more akin to the expanse of Charlemagne's Empire. The action of *The Lord of the Rings* takes place in the northwest of Middle-earth, in a region roughly equivalent to the European landmass. Hobbiton and Rivendell, as Tolkien often acknowledged, were roughly intended to be on a latitude of Oxford. By his own estimations, this put Gondor and Minas Tirith some 1000km (600 miles) to the south in a location that might be equivalent to Florence. In another letter, Tolkien states bluntly that "The progress of the tale ends in what is far more like the re-establishment of an effective Holy Roman Empire with its seat in Rome…".

The Emperor and the High King

Aragorn adds further authenticity to his claim as the true heir to the Dúnedain Kingdom by virtue of the "healing hands" of a true king. Both Charlemagne and Aragorn were credited with a charismatic power to heal and command. Also, Aragorn was marked apart from others by his Elvish knowledge of the healing properties of plants and herbs. After the Siege of Gondor, Aragorn used the herb athelas to bring Éowyn the Shield Maiden of Rohan back from the death-like trance induced by the poisoned Black Breath of the Witch King. In the Carolingian legends, Charlemagne was reputed to have been able to cure those struck down by the plague, the "Black Death", by using the herb known as sowthistle. In both cases, these herbs only worked their magical cures if administered by the healing hands of the king – acknowledged in the folklore of Middle-earth, where the common name for athelas is "kingsfoil".

There are many incidents in *The Lord of the Rings* which link the Emperor Charlemagne to Aragorn, the future King Elessar. One involves Roland, Charlemagne's most famous paladin, who makes his heroic last stand in the Roncevalles Pass in the Pyrenees while under attack by the Saracens. Ambushed and vastly outnumbered, Roland fights valiantly on until his sword breaks, and he is overwhelmed by the infidel hordes. As he dies, Roland blows his horn Oliphant to warn Charlemagne of the proximity of his foes. As Charlemagne approaches the Saracens flee, and Roland speaks but a few words before he dies. This event is comparable to the last stand of Gondor's greatest warrior, Boromir, on the cliff pass above the Rauros Falls. Ambushed by a troop of Orcs and heavily armed Uruks, Boromir blows his mighty Horn of Gondor. Aragorn, like Charlemagne, rushes to the site of the battle. Aragorn is too late to help Boromir, but hears him utter a few last words before he expires.

The tale of Boromir also echoes the Middle-earth tale of the Vala Oromë (meaning 'Hornblower'), called Araw by the Grey Elves, and Arawn in Welsh legend. And each relates to the Norse God Heimdall, as the Watchman before the Cliffs of Heaven whose horn, "Gjall", sounds the call to the Last Battle at the End of the World.

In enemies as well as allies, the Emperor and the King have much in common. At the Battle of Pelennor Fields, Gondor's allies, the Riders of the Mark meet the enemy in the form of the Southron cavalrymen of Harad. They resemble the historic enemies of Charlemagne – the Moors of Spain and the Saracens of North Africa. Other foes of Gondor were the ancient, rebellious Dunlendings who inhabited the lands below the White Mountains in ancient days, and who have their historic equivalent in the Basque mountain tribes. To the east, among the foes of Gondor were the many Easterling barbarians of Rhûn (East). Many of these wild barbarians carried shields and banners marked with the One Eye of Sauron. In historic terms these could have been pagan Lombards, Avars and Vandals, all worshippers of Odin the Necromancer, the One-Eyed God. The rulers of the many nations of the Easterlings of Rhûn were undoubtedly equivalent to the Seljuk Turks of Rhum (or Asia Minor) or the later Ottoman Turks. Among the Easterlings fighting Tolkien's forces of Gondor were the Variags of Khan. Historically, these are akin to the Variangians of the Khanate of Kiev of the (former) Khazar Empire. Worshippers of Odin, the Variangians were Norse river-raiders and -traders who drove the Khazars from Kiev, then enslaved the Slavs to work their estates. To the Slavs, they were the "Rhos", or "Rus"– and later, the Russians.

Victory over the Ring Lord allowed Aragorn to reinstate the ancient kingdoms in the Reunited Kingdom of the Dúnedain, and bring about a renaissance in art, science, music, law, and architecture. In historic times, Charlemagne was the greatest and most influential monarch of medieval Europe who finally brought some stability to the region. Charlemagne was truly the founding father of Europe. Many of Charlemagne's policies have determined the religious, linguistic and national identities of most of the people of Western Europe. Charlemagne laid down the Empire-wide feudal system of social order and rank, weights and measures, the legal system, the monetary system, and the manorial land system that would shape Europe for a thousand years.

The Holy Roman Empire also established the separate rights of Church and State, and defined roles for emperor and pope, knight and priest, villain and serf. It was also the age in which chivalry was born, that gave legal force to oaths of allegiance, and preserved German systems and values. After Charlemagne the nations of Western Europe and the idea of Europe began to emerge. Charlemagne drove back the tide of Islam, and conquered and converted virtually the whole of Europe. On Christmas Day in Rome in the year 800AD, the Pope anointed Charlemagne the first "Emperor of the Romans".

Charlemagne and the English wizard

Gandalf the Wizard was the tutor, mentor, and advisor to many kings of Elves and Men, during his thousand years of wandering the mortal lands of Middle-earth. In *The Lord of the Rings*, Gandalf appears as Aragorn's mentor, war counsellor and spiritual guide. In Charlemagne's time, a non-Christian advisor, however wise, would not have been tolerated. Historically, Charlemagne's real-life Christian "wizard" was that most remarkable English clergyman, Alcuin of York. This aristocratic English churchman was tutor, mentor, advisor and friend to Charlemagne. Alcuin brought many scholars from York and Rome to Charlemagne's court. As the Wizard Gandalf inspired Aragorn, Alcuin of York was the driving force behind the cultural revival of Northern Europe that became the Carolingian Renaissance. Alcuin was also one of the chief architects of Charlemagne's legal system, monetary system (pounds and pence), weights and measures, manorial land system, and social hierarchy.

Alcuin also wrote widely distributed tracts on the separate authorities of church and state; of bishops and kings, of emperors and popes. Alcuin alone dared to remind Charlemagne that an Emperor's authority was only borrowed from God, who decides the fate of empires. Authority demanded obligation, as Alcuin once famously wrote to the Emperor. "Do not think of yourself as a lord of the world, but a steward!" These are Alcuin's words to Charlemagne, almost identical to Gandalf's words to Denethor the Ruling Steward of Gondor. And it might have been Alcuin of York, instead of Gandalf the Wizard, who shouted: "For I am also a steward. Did you not know?" Both Alcuin the Churchman and Gandalf the Wizard had obligations far beyond the rise and fall of the petty kingdoms of mortal Men. Gandalf the Wizard was the mortal form of the immortal Maia, Olórin. And in either form, his allegiance was to the Guardians of Arda, whose authority was only borrowed from Eru Ilúvatar. Ultimately, Gandalf was steward to Eru the One, as Alcuin was steward to his One Christian God.

It was this mutually supportive but well-defined idea of a division of religious and secular power that made the alliance of divergent nations united by religion possible. As the Carolingian/Holy Roman Empire, this alliance of powers under a single emperor survived for over 1000 years. For much of that time it was Europe's most dominant cultural and political power. However, the true nature of the Holy Roman Empire was almost entirely shaped by the administration of its founder. It was Charlemagne's military, political, religious and social policies that resulted in the creation of the collective entity that became Europe.

Alcuin returned to York, again at the centre of a cultural revival that amounted to a national renaissance, especially in the publication of English books and tracts by Bede, Boethius, and others – including himself – that were read throughout the Christian World. There too, Alcuin found himself employed once again as tutor and adviser to another king. This time, it was Edwin, King of England. Alcuin saw King Edwin of the English and the Emperor Charlemagne of the Franks as two ideal princes of Christendom.

As well as culturally giving shape to modern Europe, the Carolingian/Holy Roman Empire's military strength twice saved Christian Europe from extinction. On two occasions, militant Islamic invaders threatened to put an end to Christian Europe, altogether. The first Islamic invasion was during the eighth century with the conquest of Spain, Greece and the Balkans by the Moors. Charlemagne's heavily armoured Frank cavalry was the only force capable of defeating the Moors. The battle south of Paris resulted in victory for the Franks. The defeated Islamic forces retreated over the mountains into Spain. It took generations to drive the Moors from Spain, but the tide had turned on Islam's military ambitions in Europe.

It was eight centuries later before Islamic forces attempted another invasion of Europe. This was in the sixteenth century, and this time the threat came from the east. The Holy Roman Empire of Charles V was larger and stronger than the Carolingian empire of Charlemagne's day 800 years before, but so was the enemy. Geographically the Holy Roman Empire had shifted eastward and its capital was Vienna on the Danube. Like the White Tower of Gondor, Vienna is so situated that controls all east-west and north-south traffic by road or river. Vienna was Europe's door to Asia; unfortunately, it could also be Asia's door to Europe. The Ottoman Turks decided to knock on that door – with cannonballs. Having conquered all else, the military machine of the Ottoman Empire seemed likely to conquer all Christian Europe. However, the walls of Vienna stood against the invaders, and in the end, it was the armies of the Holy Roman Empire that forced the Turks into a bloody retreat, and ended forever Islam's military ambitions in Western Europe.

Tolkien took his history seriously – and personally. The fact that the spiritual and intellectual initiative in the Holy Roman Empire had to a lrage part been provided by an Englishman, Alcuin of York, was a matter of some pride to Tolkien. If the Reunited Kingdom of the Dúnedain was comparable to the Holy Roman Empire, then the influence of Gandalf and the Elves of Rivendell over Aragorn must be comparable to the influence of Alcuin of York and the Churchmen of Rome over Charlemagne.

Tolkien saw his personal mythology linked to the Holy Roman Empire through his mother's early Mercian-English ancestors, and later through his father's Austrian-German ancestors. Just as Hobbits were chosen by Gandalf as counsellors in Aragorn's Reunited Kingdom; so Tolkien's Mercian ancestors were chosen by Alcuin as counsellors in Charlemagne's empire. And just as Hobbits became soldiers and cavalrymen in the Reunited Kingdom; so some Mercians became soldiers or cavalrymen in the imperial army.

Tolkien's ancestral connections with the Holy Roman Empire were strangely symmetrical. For as his mother's Mercian ancestors may have fought in the Imperial Army against the Moorish invasion of Europe in the eighth century, his father's ancestry is linked to the Holy Roman Empire at the time of the Ottoman Turkish invasion of Europe in the 16th century. A Tolkien family legend claimed that the "original" Tolkien had been an officer in the Imperial cavalry of the Holy Roman Empire – comparable to the Rohan cavalry, allies of the Dúnedain. His name had been George von Hohenzollern, and it was claimed he had fought alongside Archduke Ferdinand of Austria against fores of invading Turks at the Siege of Vienna in 1529. It was said that during the siege, von Hohenzollern made a series of flamboyant cavalry raids that were so outrageously dangerous, he earned the nickname "Tollkuhn", meaning "foolhardy". It was a tale Tolkien deprecated all his life, but secretly it delighted him. He often retold the tale in disguised form so obscurely that virtually none of his readers or lecture audience would register his private little joke. On several occasions he used the name "Rashbold"; while in the introduction to his famous lecture series *On Fairy Tales*, Tolkien apologized for being "Overbold", then claims to be: "Overbold by name" and "Overbold by nature".

Kings of men in glory

As already suggested, Tolkien had a number of personal reasons for creating in Aragorn a kind of prototype for Charlemagne. However, one last glance at Aragorn as King Elessar after death is also quite instructive. The King lay in state in the necropolis of Gondor in the House of Kings: "And long there he lay, an image of the splendour of the Kings of Men in glory undimmed before the breaking of the world." Aragorn is a

Above Reminiscent of *The Song of Roland*, Boromir blows a horn in vain to summon help in his fight against a band of Orcs. After his death, the remaining members of the Fellowship commit his body to the River Anduin.

king who is the very embodiment of the noble northern spirit that Tolkien so admired. In death Aragorn's face became calm and there "a great beauty was revealed in him, so that all who after came there looked on him in wonder; and the valour of his manhood, and the wisdom and majesty of his age were blended together."

One needs to remember that Aragorn took an average man's lifetime of seventy years to pass through each of the three major stages of the archetypal hero's life (birth, death, and rebirth/regeneration), and that each is an eternal "image of the splendour of Kings of Men in glory" in that timeless realm of myth. Tolkien believed that it is precisely because this image of the ideal king pre-existed in Myth Time that men of his own age were able to recognize Charlemagne as one of those "Kings of Men in glory." Or, indeed, why Charlemagne aspired to such heroic ideals in the first place.

In the warrior societies of his pagan ancestors, Tolkien saw much that was admirable: codes of honour, oaths of allegiance, astonishing acts of courage. In Charlemagne we see ancient traditions tamed and civilized by Christianity. Charlemagne was also the embodiment of the "noble spirit of the north", but unlike Aragorn, the Emperor's nobility had been sanctified and brought to a greater purpose and glory. It was in what Tolkien called the "theory of courage" that he expressed the most admiration for his ancient ancestors. Tolkien wrote of "the theory of courage, which is the greatest contribution of early Northern literature."

Life was seen as hostile, while death was something dark, cold and without consolation. The world of the ancient Anglo-Saxon gave no quarter to gods, let alone Men. Tolkien knew the Northern gods were on the side of right and nobility, but in that world that is not the team that wins. The gods and heroes are defeated by the monsters and swallowed up in the eternal dark – only tales of their heroic deeds remain (and then only as long as the tribe or the poets' words survive). As Tolkien once observed, although the gods are defeated, the rough philosophers of these peoples believed that defeat was the fate of all mortals, and eventually even the fate of the gods themselves. It was simply a matter of finding a defiant and honourable means of departing when the moment came.

This was something Tolkien would not agree with, or even wish to contemplate for himself as a Christian, but there is something curiously familiar – and contemporary – about Tolkien's discussion of his "theory of courage" as applied to Men in a pre-Christian era of darkness and chaos in a godless universe. It sounds exactly like his "theory of courage" as applied to Men in a *post*-Christian era of darkness and chaos in a Godless universe. In fact, it resonated with that indifferent universe of contemporary literature that was concerned with life after the "death of God" – 20th-century existential literature that Tolkien believed he had spent his entire life successfully avoiding.

Existential authors also looked to mythology for an analogue for the modern condition. Camus found it in the myth of Sisyphus condemned to an eternal, meaningless repetitious task without consolation or reward of any kind. As Tolkien himself acknowledged, the fate of all Men is ultimately death. And honour does not lie in victory. Honour is gained in facing life with brutal honesty and finding "a potent but terrible solution in naked will and courage." These are Tolkien's words, but they could have been the words of Camus or any of the most radical existential writers of his day. It is a philosophy that was both ancient, and – for Tolkien (a proud card-carrying old fogey since childhood) – disturbingly modern.

Selected further reading

Carpenter, Humphrey *The Inklings: CS Lewis, JRR Tolkien, Charles Williams and their Friends* (Harper Collins, 1997)
   JRR Tolkien: A Biography (Harper Collins, 2002)

Carpenter, Humphrey and Tolkien, Christopher (eds) *The Letters of JRR Tolkien* (Harper Collins, 1991)

Chance, Jane *Lord of the Rings: The Mythology of Power* (University Press of Kentucky, 2001)
   Tolkien's Art: A Mythology for England (University Press of Kentucky, 2001)

Curry, Patrick *Defending Middle-earth: Tolkien, Myth and Modernity* (Harper Collins, 1998)

Day, David *Tolkien: The Illustrated Encyclopedia* (Mitchell Beazley, 1992)

Day, David A *Tolkien Bestiary* (Mitchell Beazley, 1979)

Day, David *Tolkien's Ring* (Pavilion 1999)

Eddy Smith, Mark *Tolkien's Ordinary Virtues: Discovering the Spiritual Themes of "The Lord of the Rings"* (Inter-Varsity Press, 2002)

Foster, Robert *Complete Guide to Middle-earth* (Harper Collins, 1991)

Jones, Leslie Ellen *Myth and Middle-earth:Exploring the Medieval Legends behind JRR Tolkien's "The Lord of the Rings"* (Open Road Publishing, 2002)

Kocher, Paul *Master of Middle-earth: the Achievement of JRR Tolkien* (Pimlico, 2002)

Noel, Ruth S *The Languages of Tolkien's Middle-earth* (Houghton Mifflin, 1990)

Pearce Joseph *Tolkien: Man and Myth* (Harper Collins, 1999)

Shippey, Tom *JRR Tolkien: Author of the Century* (Harper Collins, 2001)
   The Road to Middle-earth: How JRR Tolkien created a New Mythology (Harper Collins, 1992)

Stanton, Michael N *Hobbits, Elves and Wizards: the Wonders and Worlds of JRR Tolkien's "The Lord of the Rings"* (St Martin's Press, 2001)

Tolkien, Christopher ed., The History of Middle-earth (12 volumes), (Harper Collins 1991–2002)
   The Book of Lost Tales (I); *The Book of Lost Tales* (II); *The Lays of Beleriand*; *The Shaping of Middle-earth*; *The Lost Road*; *The Return of the Shadow*; *The Treason of Isengard*;, *The War of the Ring*; *Sauron Defeated*; *Morgoth's Ring*; *The War of the Jewels*; *The Peoples of Middle-earth*; *The History of Middle-earth Index*

Tolkien JRR *The Hobbit* (Harper Collins, 1995)
   The Lord of the Rings (Harper Collins, 2002)
   The Monsters and the Critics: The Essays of JRR Tolkien (Harper Collins, 1991)
   The Silmarillion (Harper Collins, 1992)
   Tree and Leaf (Harper Collins, 2001)

Wynn Fonstad, Karen *The Atlas of Middle-earth* (Harper Collins, 1999)

Index